For Rochelle

An Improper English Mission
An Olympia Brown Mystery

by

Judith Campbell

[signature]

Mainly Murder Press, LLC
PO Box 290586
Wethersfield, CT 06129-0586
www.mainlymurderpress.com

Mainly Murder Press

Editor: Judith K. Ivie
Cover Designer: Karen A. Phillips

The cover photo featuring the Fountains Abbey in the
United Kingdom was taken by Judith Campbell.

Copyright © 2014 by Judith Campbell
Paperback ISBN 978-0-9913628-0-6
Ebook ISBN 978-0-9913628-1-3

Published in the United States of America by
Mainly Murder Press
PO Box 290586
Wethersfield, CT 06129-0586
www.MainlyMurderPress.com

Dedication

To all those beloved and respected animals who bless and grace our lives and who share our precious Mother Earth planet

As this story unfolded Thomas the cat grew into a major player and created his own persona. He is "every cat," the house pet that is a companion and a healer and a seer and who often knows us better than we know ourselves. I've always been a lover and a respecter of animals and am keenly aware of the vital role they play in so many of our lives.

This is to thank all those service dogs and monkeys; therapy horses; nursing home cats, dogs, parrots and bunnies; and those rescue animals and scraggly outcasts that follow us home and set up housekeeping in our hearts. Add to this all those beautiful and often elusive animals in the wild whose native habitat is being relentlessly and systematically destroyed by thoughtless and greedy human beings.

I donate a portion of my personal profits from the Mission Mysteries to animal welfare. If you love animals and you have enjoyed this book and some or all of my others, please join me in helping and protecting them.

In the US, you can visit www.aspca.org and www.paws.org, and in the UK you can go to https://www.ifaw.org/united-kingdom and https://www.rspca.org.uk.

Acknowledgments

First last and always, and this time specifically, an enthusiastic thank you to my English Gentleman, Chris Stokes, who interestingly enough bears an uncanny likeness to Olympia's Frederick. He is always my first reader, but on this book he's also been my invaluable English language consultant, because in this story, Olympia is really the only American voice.

Because most of the characters are English, most of the dialogue is British English. So to help American readers (and amuse my English fans) I added a dictionary of terms at the back of this book.

Thank you to my English Giggleswick writers. You know who you are, and you are right here on these pages with me. Thank you also to my 3 on 3 writers and my OBL writers, for your continuing support and honest, constructive comments. You help me make these books happen.

To my readers on both sides of the Atlantic who keep asking for more, to Karen Phillips, the designer of these fantastic covers, and Judith Ivie, my visionary and brutally honest and wickedly funny publisher, my respect, love and gratitude. This really is a team effort. Thank you, all of you.

--Judith Campbell

Praise for the Olympia Brown Mysteries

"In *A Predatory Mission,* author and minister, the Reverend Dr. Judith Campbell takes on the highly charged subject of clergy sex abuse. She writes honestly and clearly about this much talked about but poorly understood subject. She does not back away from the truth or the untoward and illustrates plainly how a predator sexually assaults those whom he was called to pastor. I have added Campbell's book as required reading, next to those of Nathaniel Hawthorne, John Updike and Sinclair Lewis, in the courses and programs I offer on clergy sexual misconduct. Like Hawthorne in *The Scarlet Letter,* Campbell writes about the real and serious damage done to people by clergy hypocrisy and abuse of power. But unlike Hawthorne, her novel is accessible and entertaining. You will not be able to put it down."

The Reverend Dr. Deborah J. Pope-Lance, minister, psychotherapist and consultant on clergy malpractice and creating safe congregations

"An Unspeakable Mission is an engaging and thought-provoking story of two dedicated and impassioned clerics struggling to find the truth when secrets and silence are the expected norms. And when 21st century religion gets involved with religious and cultural expectations of the past, the story doesn't always turn out as expected. I kept turning the pages to see what would happen next."

Rev. Keith Kron, Director of the Transitions Office for the Unitarian Universalist Association

"Judith Campbell does a superb job in the follow-up to her suspense/thriller, *A Deadly Mission,* as Olympia Brown is once again tangled up in the personal life of one of her students, an ugly secret too horrible to speak of, and a death that looks suspiciously like murder!"

Brenda Scott, Manchester Contemporary Literary Examiner,
Examiner.com

"Rev. Judith Campbell has done it again in *An Unspeakable Mission,* her second in the Olympia Brown mystery series. Using her experience as an ordained minister as well as a writer, Judith deftly weaves a compelling mystery about the death of an abusive alcoholic in a suspicious house fire, with the horrific subjects of incest and domestic violence. ...a perfect balance between building suspense and giving voice to victims who can't speak for themselves, proving in the process that what often seems obvious ... isn't."

Dawn Braash, avid reader and owner of Bunch of Grapes,
the flagship bookstore of Martha's Vineyard where
authors and readers find everything they are looking for.

~

The Olympia Brown "Mission Mystery" Series
A Deadly Mission
An Unspeakable Mission
A Despicable Mission
An Unholy Mission
A Predatory Mission
An Improper English Mission

The Moorlands

An Ecumenical Religious Retreat and Conference center
offering inspirational views of the Yorkshire Moors,
central heating and all modern conveniences,
comfortable accommodations, traditional English fare
Under **NEW** Management
**Book YOUR religious retreat, event, family reunion
or YOUR WEDDING**
For further information and to make reservations, contact
**Managing Director Celia Attison
Telephone ... 3891473418**

Website coming soon!

One

Robert Mosely first learned of his wife's all-consuming rage and the havoc it was about to wreak in their lives on a sunny day in August while the two were seated out in the garden, enjoying their afternoon tea. This was the time when they reviewed the events of the day and, along with their tea and bread and butter sandwiches, indulged in a bit of gossip about the staff and paying guests. As head caretaker and chief bookkeeper of The Moorlands, they were considered to be below the management, but as operations and administration they ranked above the housekeepers and the kitchen staff. The two had never been blessed with children, and so it was that over the years The

Moorlands, along with a succession of ginger cats always named Thomas, had become the focus of their care and attention.

On that particular day Robert was telling his wife Margery how he'd like to have a proper holiday someday, maybe a week in the Lake District or perhaps go off to one of the Channel Islands. They'd not been anywhere since their parents died; there never seemed to be extra money for such luxury. Still, he reasoned, they were happy as they were, weren't they? Their tastes and needs were simple, and employment and lodging were assured as long as The Moorlands continued as it had done all these years. Maybe it was because of an expansiveness brought on by the warmth of the sun on his back and the sense of well-being he felt at the end of a good day that he decided to approach the subject once again.

"I've been thinking," he said.

"I don't like the sound of that, Robert," said his wife.

"Just hear me out, woman. I'm thinking I fancy a proper holiday. We've never had one. If we're careful and do it at a time when it isn't too busy here, we might manage a week somewhere. What d'you think, lass?"

Margery set down her tea cup and gave him an odd look. "There's something I need to tell you."

"By the look on your face, I don't think I'm going to like it."

"Happen you will, happen you won't, but it's time you knew."

"What are you going on about, woman?"

Margery folded her arms and leaned back in her chair. "For your information I have enough money set aside to take us on holiday anywhere in the world for as long as we want and go first class with it. We just have to watch and wait a little while longer."

Robert gasped and then swallowed. "Have you gone daft? I know how much money we have. I put it in the bank every week, don't I?"

Margery lowered her voice. "There's another account in a different bank outside of England. It's got well over six hundred thousand pounds in it, maybe even more, what with interest and dividends. I know, because I deposited every penny."

He leaned forward. "Now I know you've gone daft. And just how did you manage that without me knowing it... and how did you come by it?"

Margery looked straight at her husband and said quite simply, "For lack of a better word, I stole it, every last penny of it. For the last thirty years your wife, the loyal and devoted bookkeeper to The Moorlands has been spooning off a little here and a little there that no one's ever missed. I made sure of that. Then, what with compound interest and careful reinvesting, it's grown itself into a tidy little sum."

As she continued her voice became a harsh, rasping whisper, and her eyes glittered with the anger she'd suppressed for years. "I've kept it from you all these years because there was no reason to tell you, but now there is, and it's because I'm going to need your help."

Robert looked as though he'd been punched in the chest. "If you are telling the truth, Margery, and I can't believe you are, whatever it is, I want no part of it. You love The Moorlands, and so do I. This is our life. We've nothing else but this. Have you lost your senses?"

"I said I had something to tell you, Robert. Are you going to listen, or do you want to wait until you read about it in the papers."

"Hang on a minute. If it's that serious I think I'd better have another cup of tea."

Robert Mosely dumped out the remains of the cold tea and reached for the milk jug. After he'd poured in a healthy slosh of milk, he refilled his cup, using the flowered china teapot they'd received as a wedding gift. Then he held it up and shook it in his wife's direction, but she set her mouth in a firm line and shook her head. He had a habit of stalling when he didn't want to hear something, and it never failed to irritate her.

"Are y'done faffin' about, or are y'going to have another biscuit and take up a little more time? Maybe you'd like a bacon butty to go with it, and some chips."

He shook his head, "Go on then."

"You've missed something these thirty years, Robert, and it's not just the money. I don't love The Moorlands. I hate The Moorlands, and I hate everything and everyone connected to it. It's taken me thirty years to come this far, and I'm not going to let Miss Fresh-face New-blood Celia Attison and her bloody great plan for modernization stop me now."

"But ..."

She held up her hand. "Just hear me out, will you? This is what you don't know. My grandmother was a kitchen maid in this very house when she was a girl. She was honest, and she worked hard; but it seems like the master of the house, Sir Gregory Ashton-Beckett, decided he required more than her services in the kitchen. The poor thing desperately needed the pittance they paid, and she didn't dare refuse him. Well, you know what happened, and when it did, they blamed her for seducing him and turned her out without a farthing or a character reference."

Robert shook his head. "You never told me."

"Well, I'm telling you now. Can you imagine it? Even her own parents blamed her. They said it was she who'd disgraced the family and not that titled monster of a man. She soon gave birth to my mother and was eventually married off to a pig farmer. He was a widower with six children who lived in Lancashire. Out of sight, out of mind, you might say. She had a hard life, did my mother, but she was determined to leave her own mother's shame behind her and make a better life for herself. But can you imagine what it was like with nothing but pig muck to your name, the smell of it clinging to your clothes and your hair?

"She knew Sir Gregory Ashton-Beckett was her wealthy and titled grandfather, and he lived here in The Moorlands, but she was forbidden ever to speak of it. Even when my grandmother took ill, and my mother went to him, begging for help, he wouldn't turn a hand. Said he couldn't afford to help every beggar that came to the door and sent her off in tears."

Margery blew out a breath in anger and disgust.

"Well, after her mother died, my mother left home and got a job in a local shop, where she met my father. They married and moved to Thirsk. I was their only child. But my father died when I was five, and then my mother was on her own with me to support. She worked hard and never once asked anyone for help. She was good with numbers and found work as a bookkeeper until she died. I inherited her head for figures, and when I finished school I took a job in the accounts office of a local Woolworth's. That's when I met you."

Robert nodded slowly and picked up the part of the story he knew. "After we married we came to live and work at The Moorlands, you with your head for figures and me to fix all the things that broke. By then it wasn't a private home any longer."

"That's right. It seems that the high and mighty Sir Gregory and Lady Sarah Ashton-Beckett had fallen upon hard times and could no longer afford to keep up their historic stately home. So what did they do? They were so miserable they even found a way to make bankruptcy benefit them. The old man tried giving it to the National Trust, but they didn't want it, so he gave it to the church as a tax deduction with the provision that it be used as a retreat center. What bloody cheek. He plays the part of a pious citizen when all he's doing is dumping a house he can't keep up and calling it charity. I call it hypocrisy. Welcome to The Moorlands!"

"And we've been here ever since."

"I couldn't believe my good fortune. Getting the job gave me the opportunity I'd been looking for all my life, and I didn't even have to ask for it. On that first day, the day I sat down at the secondhand desk they shoved in my direction, I began planning."

"I ..."

She held up her hand to silence him. "It's not what you think. At least it didn't start out that way. Way back when I first started working here, I wasn't thinking about revenge, I was only thinking about what was my just due."

"I don't understand," said her husband.

"Just listen, will you? My blood grandfather, Sir Gregory, never gave so much as tuppence toward the support of my mother. It was so bloody unfair. I've carried that outrage with me ever since I knew the truth of what happened. Getting the job here gave me exactly the opportunity I was looking for, a way to make it right for my mother and my grandmother before her. The way I see it, I'm the legal heir to this place and the money it will bring when it's sold. Everyone else has died off. Of course, I can never prove it, not at this late date, but I can still make it right in my own way and in my own mind, and that has been my intention since the day I came here. "

Robert sipped at his cooling tea and said nothing.

"It didn't take me long to find the folder containing the terms of the deed and the original agreement. The place is intended to be used as a religious retreat house and conference center and nothing else, not a business venture. Should it become unable to sustain itself as such, then it is to be sold, and anything left after the fees and the bills are paid is to be given to the local diocese. I suppose that way the old man thought he could buy his way back into heaven. Maybe he thought with all the money going to the church, St. Peter wouldn't notice his heart was a block of ice and his soul was as black as night. Talk about hypocrisy, using the church to relieve him of impending debt! And it just so happens that the terms of the original agreement are going to work for us now. Make no mistake, Robert Mosely, The Moorlands is going under. I've seen to that, and when it does, we're going to get it."

"And then what?" he asked softly as the unpleasant reality, along with the complete feasibility, of her plan began to take shape in his own mind.

"When the day comes, I'll find someone to buy it anonymously in my name. Then we'll go off to Spain while the estate agent we've hired sells it to an investor for a very high price. This is prime land. It's not far from the A65 and the A59 so it offers easy access to several larger cities. Bedroom communities are going up all over England. We'll sell it to the highest bidder and retire as millionaires with nobody the wiser. Then you can have your bloody holiday anywhere you want, luv, and first class with it! But not until after I come back and watch the bulldozers knock down every filthy stick and stone of this place and everything it stands for."

Margery was breathing faster now, and her dark eyes were like pointed arrows aimed directly at her husband.

"It started out with penny numbers, a little here and a little there. Then, when no one took notice, the numbers started going up. I opened an account in a Swiss bank, and I can say with some confidence that in the intervening years we have become quite wealthy. We can do what we want, just not when we want. The timing from now on is critical. When it's all done and dusted, Sir Gregory's obligation to my mother and my grandmother will be paid in full, and you and I will be far away."

Two

By the beginning of September Celia Attison had been managing director at The Moorlands for four months. She had been the board's first choice out of the final three candidates because of her outstanding qualifications, references and much needed energy and vision. They hoped she could breathe new life into the elegant but stodgy old establishment and, with their guidance and counsel, bring it into the twenty-first century.

There were, however, those within the organization who held a very different view. They felt someone from the inside should have been promoted to that position. Someone with more seniority, who knew everyone and understood how things were done there, should have been given that job. Someone who knew the governing rules of the establishment and wouldn't ask questions. Celia was not that person.

Of late, the tensions between vision and tradition, between growth and comfort, between the elevated and pushed aside, were near or at the breaking point. There was no question among some present that Celia Attison had to go, and the sooner the better. So it was that one evening when only a couple of paying guests were in residence, Margery invited a select few of the longtime staff to the Moselys' cottage for a little chat.

She carefully described the instability of the present financial situation, the real threat to all their livelihoods and the urgent need to assist Mrs. Celia Attison safely out of her position at The Moorlands.

"Nothing bad or hurtful, you understand," said Margery, looking concerned and sounding almost kindly in her approach. "She's a good woman who can't seem to understand that she shouldn't be working here. Little things have to happen that will convince her this is not the best place for her—simple blunders and minor accidents, meetings that get put off, tasks that are done wrong, things that inconvenience the guests and make her appear, uh, less than adequate to the job. Such things as never happened before she came to work here will show everyone how she's not doing the job for which she was hired. We need everyone, and in particular the board of governors, to see how seriously the place is getting away from her."

Alex Brant, the second assistant groundskeeper raised a cautious hand. "But wasn't she the one who was supposed to make it better? We all know this place has been going downhill for years. Maybe we should give her more of a chance. If The Moorlands goes under we'll all lose our jobs. Where will we be then?"

Margery spoke slowly. "No, Alex, that's just it, please try and understand. If she *stays* we'll lose our jobs. She's planning to cut staff to lower expenses. What's that going to do to us, to you and you and you?" She pointed at each of them.

He nodded, but it was clear he was not comfortable with the idea.

Margery was relentless. "The key to this is to make sure whatever it is that finally succeeds in convincing Celia to, uh, move on in no way causes any harm or points to any one thing or person. This is for the good of all of us," she assured them, all the while nodding her head to emphasize her point. "We're a team. We're the old guard. We know what works here; she doesn't. Celia Attison isn't one of us, and if you really think about it, it will be to her benefit as well. She wants to do a good job, doesn't she? Well, I say she can do a good job somewhere else, and we need to give her that opportunity. Funny thing is, I wouldn't be surprised if one day she comes back and actually thanks us."

Alex nodded doubtfully. He was still not fully convinced, but he was willing to join the effort.

Margery Mosely knew job security and tradition were on their side, but time was not. She remembered a line from *Macbeth* she had read as a schoolgirl: "If it were done when 'tis done, then 'twere well it were done quickly."

She smiled almost benignly as she made her final summary. "The point is, Celia never should have been given the job in the first place. She can't do it. It's a cruelty, really, to let her keep struggling, but the board doesn't see it that way, so in the end, if we want to preserve our life here, it's going to be up to us to make it happen."

She was answered by a few nods and murmurs of cautious assent as she looked down and squinted at the pendant watch pinned to her blouse. "Goodness me, I've kept us all up far too late. If any of you have thoughts or ideas on the matter, come and have a word with me. The fact is our dear Mrs. Attison is simply not of the quality required for The Moorlands. She will either bankrupt this place before our very eyes, or it will happen by itself, and she will try and blame us. I'm afraid we have no choice but to see that she doesn't have the chance to do either. Come on, Robert, it's time to give our Thomas his supper and let these good people go to their beds."

Margery Mosely had come a long way from her days as the shy and awkward granddaughter of the disgraced wife of a Lancashire pig farmer. No one, not Celia Attison or even her good solid husband Robert, was going to deter her from her mission.

Frederick looked up from his book as his newly espoused wife entered the room. "Who was that on the phone, my love?"

"You aren't going to believe this," said the Reverend Doctor Olympia Brown.

"I'm not going to believe what?"

"How do you fancy a trip to England?"

He put down the book.

"That was Richard Attison, my minister-friend from the UK. He's asked if I'd like to come over and be on the teaching staff of a church leadership seminar he's doing."

Frederick leaned back in the chair and crossed his arms. "Hang on a minute. Out of the blue, a friend you haven't seen for years just up and calls you and asks you to come over there and teach a course. Now why don't you tell me the rest of the story, because I know there is one."

"Funny you should ask."

"I'm waiting," said Frederick.

"Well, there seems to be something nasty going on at a certain religious retreat house in West Yorkshire where his wife Celia is the Managing Director."

"Such as?"

"That's what he'd like me to find out. He thinks someone there, possibly one the staff members, has taken against her and is trying to making life so miserable that she'll resign, and they can be rid of her."

Frederick was looking less convinced and more skeptical by the minute. "That sort of thing happens all the time in business. It's mean spirited, but it's not new. How is this particular campaign being made manifest, and why is it so bad that he thinks you should make an appearance?"

"Richard said that lately, all sorts of things have mysteriously and inconveniently gone wrong—toilets backing up, power going out, reservations getting lost, and staff calling in sick more and more frequently or not turning up at all. Last month the freezer quit on the weekend before a huge posh wedding, and all the food was spoiled. His wife is beginning to think some of these occurrences are neither accidental nor coincidental, but rather there's an organized effort on the part of one or some of the longtime staff to make her look incompetent. He says it's like the plagues of Egypt with each successive unfortunate incident getting more pointed and more damaging.

And we all know what the last plague was, although I think I might be carrying the metaphor a bit too far."

"Crikey," said Frederick, "and just what does he think you'd be able to do in such nefarious circumstances?"

"He thinks if a total outsider, someone with no knowledge of the history of the place or the interpersonal dynamics of the people involved, were to come and do a little …"

"Skulking around?" finished Frederick.

"Well, something of the sort. He thinks I might see things that others don't and ask the kinds of questions that proper English people would never think to ask."

"Oh, you'd do that, all right. I'm not entirely sure if England's green and pleasant land is ready for the likes of you, my dear."

"Whatever do you mean?"

"I mean that you do fit some of the stereotypes we English hold deep in our hearts about you Yanks."

"Such as?"

"No offense, Reverend Lady, but you never hesitate, even for a moment, to say what you think. You often go where you shouldn't go, and you don't ever take no for an answer, and that's only chapter one."

"And you think there's something wrong with that?"

"Certainly not in your way of seeing things. However, it might rather dismay the landed gentry for you to hit them full bore without proper warning. You are rather a force of nature, you know."

"All of that notwithstanding, what do you think?"

"Think about what?"

Olympia made a face. "This is getting circular. I started all of this by asking if you wanted to go to England for a couple of weeks."

At first Frederick looked resigned, and then he brightened. "I say, we never had a proper English honeymoon. If we were to go, I could take you to meet the family."

"Frederick, we've only been married for six weeks."

He gasped and clapped the back of his hand to his brow. "Is that all? It seems like forever."

"Frederick!"

He winked at her. "Call your friend Richard back and find out more of what he's thinking. If he can make arrangements to put us up, I can probably get a couple of weeks off from the bookstore. You don't have a church commitment in the immediate future, so as long as we can arrange cat care, there's nothing to hold us back. Someone's got to look after you, and I do speak the language."

"Very funny, but let me sleep on it. Actually, I think I'll check in with Miss Winslow, as well," said Olympia.

"As our resident house-ghost in charge of looking after us, she doesn't exactly come to call, you know."

"No, Frederick, I mean I'll just take a couple of minutes and read a few pages in the diary I found when I first moved into this house. It's amazing how her life of a hundred and sixty years ago has so many parallels to my own. Not word for word, mind you, but in her vision and her ways of thinking. I wish I could have known her."

"Ah, my love, but I think on some cosmic level you know each other very well."

As Frederick picked up his latest *Guardian* crossword, and Olympia reached for the diary, the clock on the mantel, the one that didn't work, chimed not once but twice.

"Well, fancy that," said Frederick. "If I'm not mistaken, she's getting positively conversational."

November 4, 1862
The leaves have almost all fallen now, and the bare branches creak and snap in cold November wind. No doubt winter will soon be upon us, and we are well prepared. How good it is to be back in my own home. The two months I spent in Cambridge

with Aunt Louisa were most productive. With her to care for little Jonathan, I was able to make significant progress on my first novel, Bright Days, Dark Nights. *In many ways it is like writing a second diary; I find myself time and time again writing my own story. I suppose this is what all writers do, and I can safely hide behind my pseudonym, CK Barrow. Only Aunt Louisa and my dear neighbor, Richard Fuller, know the truth, and they have sworn to keep my secret safe.*

My darling Jonathan is almost two and has enough energy for all of us. He talks like a little boy now and no longer a baby, although I must say his favorite word is still no.

But I am chattering. I confess to having a problem and no immediate solution. My child needs playmates, and I need adults with whom I might keep company and befriend. I am fond of my own company, but Aunt Louisa suggested I might be too fond of it.

Richard, my kindly neighbor, has become a very good friend, but it is awkward to go out in public with him because we are both unmarried. And while I do not live in a town of gossips, people can assume things which I would prefer they did not. I am not inclined to marry, nor is he. There must be a way for a man and a woman to be simply friends.

More anon, LFW

Three

Celia Attison locked the office door behind her, sat down at the desk and began massaging her temples. She was not going to let this get the best of her. She'd managed to hang on this long, and the last thing she'd do would be to let them see any sign of weakness. Then she whimpered as another spasm twisted her stomach. She'd been having violent spells of cramps and diarrhea for the last several days, but today of all days she could not call in sick. Celia opened the lower drawer of her desk, took out her ever-present bottle of Imodium tablets and swallowed one. That should get her through the morning and the board meeting she'd been dreading. After that, who knew? But today she would start asking questions. Somebody had to. After that … well, there was no telling, was there?

She was startled by a tap at the door.

"Are you in there, Mrs. Attison? I've brought you a cup of tea."

It was Annette Darcie, one of the newer hires in the hospitality staff. Celia stood up and opened the door. "Oh, thank you, Annette. How did you know that's just what I needed?"

Annette smiled shyly. She was an earnest young mother from the village who had applied for some part-time work while the children were at school. She worked hard and seemed eager to please. Celia worked her pained face into a weak smile and invited her to sit down.

"Well, I notice that you usually come into the kitchen before you start your day. I saw your car parked outside, and I was in the dining room setting tables, and I never saw you come in, so I thought I might bring you a cup." She lowered her voice. "And to be honest, the cook's in a fair fury, she is, and I was just as glad to get out of her way for a while." She held out the cup and saucer to Celia and then reached down into her apron pocket. "I brought you a couple of biscuits, as well, just in case you might be a bit peckish."

Even though she wasn't hungry, Celia gratefully accepted the biscuits and turned back to her desk so that Annette would not see the tears of gratitude welling up in her eyes.

"Can I get you anything else, Mrs. Attison?"

Celia smiled and shook her head. "Not that I can think of, Annette. You should probably get back to setting your tables for lunch."

Annette rolled her eyes and asked, "Shall I check in later?"

"Maybe after the board meeting this morning; it's quite possible I might need a little something."

Later on that same day Robert Mosely called his wife Margery into The Moorlands' sitting room on the pretext of pointing out a small crack in one of the windows that needed repairing. From where they were standing they could see anyone entering the room, as well as anyone passing by outside, and thus be assured they would not be overheard.

He spoke in a low voice. "I need a word."

"You look pretty grim, luv, is there a problem?"

"The short answer is yes; the longer answer is what I think needs to be done about it."

Margery leaned closer and dropped her voice. "What seems to be the trouble? I thought we were pretty much on schedule. Celia's definitely showing the strain. We've had several complaints from the board and the guests about inefficiency and poor service. Annette, the new dining room manager, was overheard to say that Celia became completely undone when she learned the staff meeting had been cancelled without her knowledge or permission."

Mosely stepped closer and made a great show of pointing to the corner of the window where the offending crack was supposedly located. Margery bent closer to examine it.

"That's just it. One of the kitchen staff told me Annette overheard Celia say that if she didn't know better, she might think people were deliberately trying to make her look bad so she'd resign."

"Well, that's exactly what we're trying to do, isn't it, make her look incompetent so she'll either resign or get fired. It's much less awkward that way. It has to look like it's her decision. She knew the place was failing when she was hired. She was supposed to be the answer to everyone's prayers. It's not our fault if she's not up to the task."

Margery blew out a little puff of irritation and then continued. "I can't help it if things didn't work out as planned. Who would have thought she'd be so high minded and mulish? We got stuck with her because Michael Herlihy changed his vote at the last minute. We were supposed to have promoted Penelope Long, the office administrator, to the position. Then the board changed direction and insisted we needed fresh blood. Well, they'll get their fresh blood all right."

"I'm not sure if I like the sound of that. Exactly what are you talking about?"

Margery dropped her voice even further. "I didn't want to rush this, but we may not have a choice. I haven't said anything to the others, but I talked to Penelope, and she says Cecilia's starting to ask more questions, serious questions. She said that if the finances are as bad as they appear, then maybe they should arrange for a full audit. That's why we cancelled the meeting this morning. If she does that, the whole thing could come undone before our very eyes. There is another very unpleasant aspect to all of this."

"And what's that, luv?" he asked.

"I've been very careful, Robert. Anyone looking into the accounts will not find any irregularities."

"What's the problem then?"

"A really clever person might start checking with the vendors and the utility people and comparing our figures to theirs."

"And then what?"

"Then there could be trouble. If someone sees that the names and figures don't match up and traces it back to me, I could be sent to prison, and they could be taking a good look at you, as well, as my husband."

"Bloody hell! I never thought of that."

"Well, I have, and it's not something I fancy. We're too far along. This place will be worth millions in a year or two, and when that happens, it needs to be ours."

Robert nodded in agreement. "So we need to speed this whole thing along before she asks any more questions, and once she's gone, then what?"

Robert was not a creative thinker, but he was an excellent first mate, and he knew how to follow directions. He would never have considered anything remotely like this on his own, but once he saw the logic of her idea and the need to have steady employment and keep a roof over their heads, he was soon convinced.

"Then I offer to step in and hold the office and the books together just like I did when the last manager left and before they hired Celia. I'm the only person here who knows that The Moorlands is within two months of bankruptcy. If we can be rid of her by the end of this month, then I'm still on schedule, and the place will be ours.

"But that's less than a fortnight."

"Margery nodded. " That's right, and once we own it free and clear, we put it on the market. It's all in the by-laws. I've memorized it. 'If for good and sufficient reason The Moorlands can no longer function as it was originally chartered, the board of governors shall have the power to dissolve the trust and sell the property to the highest bidder. Any funds remaining after all accounts are settled shall be given to the diocese."

Robert pulled at his chin and made a rumbling sound at the back of his throat. He did this when he was thinking about something that needed fixing. He was a methodical man who, given enough time to ponder his options, could be counted upon to sort out the most complicated of problems. Then his frown deepened. He shoved his big, rough hands into his pockets and rumbled again.

"You are thinking about something, Robert, I can always tell."

"I'm thinking that sometimes ... accidents happen."

"And just what kind of accident were you thinking about?" asked Margery.

"Something that no one would be expecting, is easy to arrange and sends Celia the final message that this is not a good place for her. Think about it. I've fixed everything around here from garden swings to tractors. I know where everything is and how it works inside this place and out and about on the grounds. If that isn't enough, I know a good bit about the insides and undersides of automobiles, as well."

Margery gasped. "Ohhh, I dunno. We can't have anything point directly to you. Something going wrong on one of the cars would do just that."

"Not so. Just little inconveniences—a broken lock, a dead battery or a flat tire—things that make her look careless and thoughtless and keep her distracted. She might have a newer car than I'm used to, but some things are still pretty basic to any vehicle. "

"And if that doesn't work?"

They were interrupted when the lounge door opened and Celia Attison entered the room. It was clear from her stride and the set of her mouth she was angry.

"Oh, there you are Margery. Have you any idea who cancelled the staff meeting today? I went up to the conference room just now, and it was dark and cold as charity. Where is everybody, and why wasn't I told?"

Margery was the picture of distressed innocence. "Oh, I do apologize, Mrs. Attison. It must have gone right out of my head. Cook came into my office this morning while you were out and told me something had come up at the last minute and she couldn't be there. You said it was mandatory that everyone be present, so I went ahead and cancelled, and I must have forgotten to tell you. That was silly of me, wasn't it? I am sorry about that. I should have asked you, but you'd been so adamant about all of us being in attendance that I thought I was doing you a favor. I suppose we'll just have to reschedule now, won't we?"

She smiled sweetly in Celia's direction. "You look like you could use a cup of tea. I know I could." Then she added, "And you, Mr. Mosely, you can go back to that tool box you were telling me about. There's always something that needs work around here, isn't there?"

Although she was less than willing to sit at the same table with Margery Mosely, Celia knew that appearances must be maintained. She could not have outright warfare now, so she went with Margery to the dining room. They were greeted by Annette Darcie, who settled them at the nearest table and brought over a tray with two cups of tea and a plate of biscuits.

"Will you have a biscuit with your tea, Mrs. Attison?" Margery held out a plate.

"No, thank you, Mrs. Mosely, just the tea, thank you. My tum's been a bit dickey these last few days."

"Aye, there's been a bit of that going around."

Four

Three weeks after the idea of going to England had first been mentioned, Olympia and Frederick were squashed into two British Airways economy class seats, doing their best to eat an airplane meal without moving their elbows. Their travel plan was to fly into Heathrow, rent a car and visit family in the south for a couple of days, then drive north to The Moorlands for the retreat week. After that they would finish up in the northeast of England, visiting more family, and then fly back to Boston out of Newcastle-upon-Tyne. It had been some time since Olympia had been in England, and she was really looking forward to seeing it through the eyes, and with the expert guidance, of a native son, AKA her new husband. She was still getting used to the sound of that word, but each day it got easier.

Their wedding had been a small one with her best friend, Fr. Jim Sawicki, serving as both officiant and best man and her daughter Laura as best woman. The only other people in attendance had been Olympia's two sons and their significant others, Laura's adoptive mother and father, and baby Erica as an in-arms flower girl.

Initially they'd wanted to hold the ceremony in mid-October, but when Olympia's daughter announced that she really wanted to be there, they moved it up to the first Sunday in September. There in Olympia's and Frederick's back yard, accompanied by cheers and tears and lots of really good champagne, they tied the knot. Two days after that Olympia was on the road to California with her daughter and granddaughter in an almost new, ruby red minivan that was Frederick's gift to Laura and Erica.

She flew back to Brookfield three weeks after that to officiate at her elder son Malcolm's wedding. It had been a very full fall, and to all appearances, as the 747 hummed along above the clouds, the momentum was going to continue for a while longer.

Frederick collected and stacked their dinner things, handed them up to the attendant and asked for refills on their coffee and tea. With the insubstantial plastic cups in hand, they settled back and prepared to try to enjoy their flight.

"Are you going to watch a movie?" asked Frederick.

"No, I don't think so, not now anyway. I brought a book and some knitting and my notes for the workshop I'm supposed to be doing. I thought I'd start with that while I'm relatively alert."

"What is it is exactly that Richard wants you to do?"

"That will require a twofold answer."

Frederick turned toward her as far as the cramped seat and tightly fastened seatbelt would allow. "I have exactly four hours and thirty-seven minutes remaining to listen."

Olympia chuckled. "Well, it would seem that almost from the time his wife Celia took the position of managing director of the retreat center, silly things have been happening and going wrong. He thinks she might have crossed swords with someone early on, and whoever it might be is trying to get back at her, or it could be more serious, and someone is actually trying to get her to quit. It's not clear."

"And what does Richard see as your part in all of this?"

Olympia finished her coffee and set the empty cup on top of Frederick's.

"Richard's been after me for some time to do something for the church leadership over there. He thinks it might be good for the British Unitarians to see what the Americans are doing in that area and *vice versa.* You know, different voice, new ideas sort of thing. He also thinks because I'm an outsider, the powers that be at the retreat center won't take me as seriously as they would one of their own. He said they might be more inclined to let down their guard and talk more freely around me, because in seven days I'll be gone."

"That may or may not be true. What does he think you might be able to accomplish in seven days? It's not very much time."

"Keep my eyes and ears open, ask what questions I can and see if I can get anyone to talk to me. There is one thing that bothers me, though. He made it very clear that he doesn't want me to breathe a word of what I'm doing on the side to his wife Celia."

"That could be rather awkward. Why ever not?"

"He says it's because she's bound and determined to handle this herself and not to let whoever is set against her know she's worried. You know, stiff upper lip and all that. This is the job of her dreams. It's a real step up for her professionally, and she's made it almost a mission to go it on her own and not buckle under or ask for help."

Frederick shook his head. "I'm not liking the sound of this, Olympia."

"You never do."

"And with good reason, I might add."

Olympia made a face. "Don't start, Frederick. As it happens I don't either, and that's precisely why I agreed to go. This kind of thing happens with revolting regularity in organizations. I witnessed it when I was teaching at Meriwether, and I've seen it play out in any number of churches. Somebody takes against the new minister or department head or CEO and pulls every trick from silent stonewalling to actual sabotage to discredit them and get them out."

"I thought this was a religious retreat center. It's hard to imagine such evil doings in a place that is supposedly doing the work of God."

"Don't kid yourself, Frederick, they can be the worst— small, inbred organizations made up of warring cliques and subsets, all with personal and sometimes toxic agendas. Talk about hypocrisy."

"How bad is it getting at The Moorlands?" asked Frederick.

"It would appear to be getting downright ugly; that's why Richard called me."

They were interrupted from further discussion by the flight attendant collecting their cups and napkins. With these cleared away Frederick and Olympia settled in for the long haul. Within minutes he was snoring softly, and Olympia was trying to sift through the clutter of papers and notes in her lap without elbowing people on either side of her.

At this point, anyway, the outline Richard had sent her looked pretty straightforward. She and Richard would start by comparing and contrasting lay and professional leadership roles and training opportunities in English churches with those of the US. Then, for a change of pace, they would look at a video she was able to get from headquarters, showing some very exciting and innovative worship ideas from some of the more forward-thinking congregations in the US. They would follow that with discussions and interactive workshops and the inevitable next-steps focus groups.

She was really getting into it when Frederick snorted, blinked, sat up and said, "I've got it!"

"You've got what?" she asked.

"A really good idea."

"Are you going to share it, or is this some new variant of twenty questions?"

Frederick straightened up and shifted into a more comfortable position. He had the look of a very smug Englishman about him.

"I suggest that while you and Richard are doing your retreating, I could be the one on the lookout. Think about it. You are the visiting dignitary. You are coming to share your wisdom and expertise while I, the humble helpmate, will appear to be sitting off to the side doing crosswords or puttering about the garden or frequenting the teapot. In reality I will be poking about and chatting up the staff. As I said before, I do speak the language. Who would ever think I was there in the role of a spy? You are an outsider and therefore could be considered a little suspect, especially because you are a friend of Richard. But I'm only the loyal English spouse who has apparently come along for a free trip home. They'd see me as part of the wallpaper and never give me a second thought."

"That is absitively brilliant," said Olympia.

"Surely you mean absolutely," said Frederick.

"Surely I don't," said Olympia.

They were interrupted by the man sitting in the window seat, who had to go to the bathroom. This involved both of them wiggling out of their seats and standing in the aisle and stretching various parts of their anatomy until he returned. Olympia decided she needed a little walkabout and left Frederick standing in the loo-line while she took a couple of turns around the steerage end of the plane. It was a day flight, so most people were either on their computers or reading as the silver leviathan thundered along. Even though Olympia knew enough about the mechanics and aerodynamics of flying to understand how the whole thing happened, she never got over the thrill of feeling the monster of a machine lift off the runway and soar into the sky. Now she was threading her way along the aisles, thirty-nine thousand feet high somewhere over the Atlantic, and wondering what on earth she would find when she landed.

It was not only the potential skullduggery at The Moorlands that was causing her some anxiety. She was also about to meet her new family, brother and sisters-in-law, nieces and nephews, in-laws and outlaws, all of them unknown quantities. What had Frederick told them about her? How would they receive this outspoken Yankee? She hoped she would pass muster, and they would not find her wanting. Time would tell, but she hoped for Frederick's sake it would all go well and she'd make him proud, and they would accept her as one of their own.

She was surprised to realize how much she wanted their approval, but it was not something she could do very much about. With her legs sufficiently stretched and the possibility of a short nap before someone started serving food again, Olympia sidled into her seat and snapped herself into place.

The remainder of the flight was blessedly uneventful. Airplane meals and cramped quarters always played havoc with her midsection, so by the time the attendants were preparing the pre-landing tea and biscuits; Olympia needed another full-body stretch and a quiet walk to a less populated part of the plane. When she returned and clambered back into her seat over a smiling Frederick, she was ready for something to eat and even more ready to be out of the plane and feel the solid English soil beneath her feet.

While the original plan had been to visit the southern branch of Frederick's family for a few days and then head north to The Moorlands, a phone call from his sister the day before they left changed everything. It had been decided by the powers that be that it might more expedient for all concerned if Olympia and Frederick waited to visit the family until after the retreat. That way, everyone would go north and stay a few days at the country home of Frederick's sister, Jenny Elder. Then, they said, Frederick's new wife could be properly introduced to the entire family at one go. More efficient that way, they told him on the long distance phone call that left him nothing else to say on the matter other than, "Jolly good."

Olympia hardly thought of herself as a shrinking violet or anything close to it, but the thought of fifteen to twenty newly acquired relatives all giving her the once-over was just the teensiest bit disquieting. This unease was not something she planned to share with Frederick. I am what I am, she told herself. I will cross my legs at the ankles, drink my tea with milk poured in the cup first and try hard not to swear.

In the end she had no choice but to agree that the overhauled plan was more efficient and a just and welcome cause for a long overdue family reunion, but the change in plans left Olympia and

Frederick with three unscheduled days before they were expected to check in at The Moorlands.

"I think we should just get into that hire-car and see where it takes us," said Frederick. I can show you bits of England that tourists will never see."

And from which I may never return, thought Olympia. The idea did not inspire a surfeit of confidence. She had, in their brief time together, learned that Frederick had the sense of direction of a dust mop. She turned and smiled innocently at him.

"I have a different idea. Let's get a road map and plan something out. I know almost nothing about the real England, and since you are a native son, who better than you to find places we could enjoy together? That way we won't be floundering around in the dark on roads we don't know. We can aim for a town or a village that is in the direction of where we are going and find a B&B for tonight. Then Friday, which is tomorrow, we can show up at The Moorlands sometime instead of Sunday."

"But they won't be expecting us. They might not have a room for us. That could be a bit awkward," said Frederick.

"My point exactly. If we turn up when they aren't ready for us, we get a chance to see them without their party faces on and see how they handle the unscripted and unexpected."

"What if they don't have an empty room?"

"We'll just find ourselves a B&B and come back when we are expected."

"You're not just a pretty face, are you?" said Frederick.

"You've only just noticed," said Olympia. To emphasize her multiple talents, she turned toward Frederick and kissed him on the cheek, then ran her hand up the inside of his leg. Frederick gasped in mock shock and then, with a familiar gleam in his eye, suggested that perhaps it might be better to spend the night at a nearby airport hotel so they could get an early start in the morning.

Five

By day two of their meandering drive, Olympia was no longer stamping on her nonexistent brake and diving to the left every time an oncoming car careened into view. The twisting, narrow, stone-walled lanes were becoming familiar, and now that she was no longer terrified, she could appreciate their timeworn asymmetry. As they drove along she could imagine the generations of families who had lived their lives in and around these hills and villages. It was clear that Frederick had not lost his driving skills and was completely in his element, zipping along sometimes only inches from gateposts and the corners of buildings and then, when duty and courtesy required, screeching to a halt and backing up so another equally intrepid driver could pass on the right.

These were places Olympia had never seen during her first trip to England. Towns and villages with names like Goosnargh, Bolton-by-Bowland and Coniston Cold came and went along with vegetarian ploughman's lunches, real steak and kidney pies for Frederick, gallons of hot strong tea and more measured pints of warm, dark brown, bitter ale. By then they were more than ready to get out of the car, stretch any body part that could move and enjoy more than forty-five minutes in a single postal code.

By teatime on Friday they were approaching Little Humblesby and looking for names of streets and signposts that would direct them to The Moorlands. The village itself was a one-street assemblage of terraces on one side of the road and several semi-detached houses on the other. It had grown up near the larger cities of Ilkley and Otley and boasted a Norman church and a half-timbered public house.

"This is picturebook quaint," squealed a delighted Olympia. "I can't believe it. Add some snow, and you'd have an English Victorian Christmas card."

"As much as some of the more affluent villages are striving to hold back the tide of progress, I'm afraid a lot of this is going the way of the buggy whip. More and more people here are leaving these quaint and hard-to-heat cottages for larger homes with more modern conveniences, larger gardens and easy access to the motorways."

"That seems a shame. I'd hate to see this lost, and I'm not even English."

"Well, I suppose you might say you are English by injection."

It took Olympia a moment to catch on, and when she did, she smacked him on the leg nearest her.

"Don't get sidetracked, my dear, we're trying to find a huge old Victorian pile calling itself The Moorlands. There, I see the street, Windy Bank Lane, turn right."

Frederick flipped on the directional signal, swung the wheel to the right in one motion and began the ascent up the narrow dirt lane. They drove slowly, turning this way and that for almost two miles before the road widened and The Moorlands came into view.

"It looks just like the picture," said an awestruck Olympia.

"It's called truth in advertising. They wouldn't exactly use a picture of Buckingham Palace, now, would they? It's got one hell of a view, though. Three hundred and sixty degrees of sheep studded, gorse flecked, rolling moorland as far as the eye can see."

Olympia was momentarily and uncharacteristically speechless.

"Didn't your friend Richard Attison say there was parking for The Moorlands staff and conference leaders around to the back? Look, there's a sign that says deliveries with an arrow pointing left."

Frederick drove slowly and carefully around the building and found the parking area marked for the staff. The minute he stopped, Olympia was out of the car, eager to look around and breathe some fresh air. Frederick was right, the view was staggering, but when she turned and looked back at the edifice at the center of it all, even from the parking lot she could see the unmistakable signs of age and neglect. She saw stone walls that needed re-pointing, ivy all but obliterating many of the windows. If the outside is in need of this much repair, she wondered, I can only imagine what's going on inside. Olympia shook off the thought for the time being. There was too much to see, too much to take in, and she wanted to do it all right now.

"Let's go and see if they have a room available before we unload our bags," suggested Frederick.

"What a good idea," said Olympia.

The front side of the building looked considerably better than the back, which most paying guests didn't see. The great studded oak door swung easily on strong, well-oiled hinges, and a big sign on a stand in the entryway welcomed guests and asked all visitors to please report to the office.

"I wonder what we should do now?" asked Frederick.

"Well, I can hear voices and the clatter of dishes coming from somewhere off to the left. Let's follow our ears and see what we find."

From her spot near the dish cupboard, Annette Darcie looked up to see Frederick and Olympia standing in the doorway to the dining room. They were not part of the group of ramblers that were there for the weekend, and she wondered who they might be. She crossed the room and held out her hand.

"Hello, there. I'm Mrs. Darcie, may I be of assistance? Dinner won't be for a while yet, but if you fancy a cup of tea and a biscuit, I can get it for you."

Frederick extended his hand. "I'm Frederick Watkins, and this is my wife, The Reverend Olympia Brown. We're booked in here for the conference that starts on Sunday, but we decided to come early and see if there might be a room available for tonight and tomorrow. We thought we could go off and do a bit of walking before then."

"Mrs. Attison has left for the day, but I think Mrs. Mosely, she's the bookkeeper, might still be in her office. She often fills in when Mrs. Attison isn't here. I know we're not full, so it's just a question of finding a room that's been made up and ready. Let me go and see if I can find her, and then I'll come back and get you that tea."

"Well, that's about as nice a welcoming as it gets," said Olympia. "No complaints there."

Frederick lowered his voice to almost a whisper. "You did say Richard wasn't entirely convinced there was anything specific going on. Isn't that why he wanted someone with a different perspective who doesn't know any of the players to come and have a bit of a look round?"

They were prevented from saying any more when Annette returned with a dark-haired woman of middling age and shape, whom she introduced as Margery Mosely.

"Do I detect an American accent then, Reverend Brown?"

"You do indeed. I'm afraid I haven't been married to this gentleman long enough to soften some of the edges of it."

This produced a perfunctory smile and the invitation to Frederick and Olympia to follow her back to the office.

"Mrs. Attison, the center director, leaves me in charge when she's gone off. Good thing it is, too; otherwise we might not have been able to accommodate you. The housekeeping staff is not authorized to book anyone in. I just happened to be working late today so I could finish up the accounts without interruption. I do that sometimes."

Margery pulled out an impressive collection of keys, located the proper one and unlocked the door marked Centre Director. Once inside she sat down at the desk, retrieved the guest register from its spot on the far corner and opened it.

"Oh, yes, here you are; Watkins and Brown, that's you lot, isn't it? It says you are arriving at teatime on Sunday."

Olympia nodded, and Frederick quipped, "That's us. We just got married, but I refused to change my name."

This produced a second thin smile. "There's a bit of luck. It seems that the room she reserved for you is unoccupied and already made up, so I can take you there directly. Then you can bring in your bags."

Frederick inclined his head with the inborn grace of the English middle class. "Yes, please do show us the room, Mrs. Mosely, but if you don't mind, I think we might have the cup of tea Mrs. Darcie offered us before we bring in our cases. We've been on the road for a couple of hours, and to be honest, I think I'd like to sit down in front of a cup of tea and a biscuit before I do anything that requires muscles."

Margery closed the book and stood. "Of course, Mr. Watkins. First we'll see the room, and then I'll ask for some tea for the two of you. Come through. Dinner will be at half-six. I'll let cook know there'll be two more for supper."

"My wife's vegetarian," said Frederick. "I hope that's not going to be a problem? I'm not sure if we mentioned that when we booked."

Margery spoke over shoulder. "I didn't see anything in the register. It's more than likely Mrs. Attison forgot to write it down. She means well, but there's just so much to remember, and she's still pretty new. It's a good job I'm here. I'll go and tell cook. Between us, I'll make sure you have something."

"That's kind of you," said a grateful Olympia.

"Most of us know how to do our jobs here, Reverend, not like some I might mention. But never mind that. If you need anything, just come straight to me, and I'll see to it. Ah, here we are." Margery stopped and pushed open the door to room 104. The loo's at the end of the hall, and we always keep a light on in the hallways. You'll find towels on the bed and extra pillows and blankets in the wardrobe."

"Wardrobe?" Olympia turned a questioning eye to Frederick.

"It's English for clothes closet, darling. I'm afraid she still doesn't speak the language, Mrs. Mosely, but we're working on it."

"Ah, Reverend Brown, it takes years. There's English English and then there's Yorkshire English, and from the sound of him, your husband's a Geordie. Now that's another language completely." She stopped and rattled through her keys a second time and finally held the proper one out to Frederick. "Here you are. I'm off to speak to cook. Can you find your way back to the dining room? Oh, and shall I call Mrs. Attison and tell her you've come in early?"

Frederick responded quickly. "That's kind of you, Mrs. Mosely, but it's not necessary. You've taken care of everything. Let her have her weekend, and don't worry about us. What with planes and hire-cars we've been sitting for the better part of three and a half days. We need to walk out in the fresh air more than we need anything else. "

"Let's hope it doesn't rain then," said Margery.

After the dour woman left Frederick closed the door behind her and stretched out on the bed nearest the window. Olympia remained standing and had a quick look around. The room was small (the brochure would describe it as cozy) with three white painted walls and the wall behind the beds covered in a flowered chintz-patterned wallpaper. The two beds were made up with plain white duvets and fat square pillows propped at an angle against the headboards. A simple desk, chair and reading lamp, the double wardrobe and a nightstand between the beds completed the furnishings. At first appearance it was clean, functional and inviting. Later they would see the patched wiring, notice the cracks in the plaster and feel a constant breeze through the single glazed ill-fitting window.

"Your initial impressions, Madame," asked Frederick

"If you're asking me if anything negative jumps out at me, the answer is no. Mrs. Mosely is a bit of a misery, but some people are just negative by nature. She may be one of those, but she got the job done. That's what really matters doesn't it? What are your thoughts?"

"The woman in the dining room who offered us tea when we got here certainly went out of her way to be welcoming. The room is clean and comfortable, and they didn't make a fuss about our getting here early, so I guess the answer is so far so good … maybe."

Six

In her new apartment in San Jose, California, Laura Wiltstrom, Olympia's daughter and oldest child, was lying in bed, staring at the ceiling. She was wondering what in the world she'd been thinking when she accepted a job on the West Coast with only her daughter for company. Little Erica, now almost a year old, had been asleep for hours in the room across the hall. Despite both Laura's biological and adoptive mothers' concerns, the child had settled in well. Laura was more than pleased with the company-provided daycare and health benefits. So what was keeping her awake? Her baby was healthy and would be taking her first steps within the week, first steps that the proud grandmothers and grandfather would not see, she reminded herself. The digital clock read 2:03 a.m.

Her job was great, and her new colleagues, while initially cautious with the eastern newcomer, were warming up and even inviting her to have lunch with them. Evenings were still spent making supper, emptying boxes and then falling exhausted into bed ... alone. Not that she was particularly interested in having a social life at the moment, but maybe after Christmas she'd think about it.

Laura Wiltstrom, the daughter Olympia Brown had been forced to give up for adoption when she was only seventeen, was lonely. She and her biological mother had only recently reconnected, and it seemed as if they were only just getting acquainted when Laura had been offered this terrific job. To refuse it would have been insane. But right now, lying flat on her back in a dark room that was three thousand miles from her adoptive family and six thousand away from her biological mother, Laura was having second thoughts. Buyer's remorse, she asked herself? Was the newness wearing off and reality hitting her like, what was it she'd heard Frederick say? "Like a slap across the belly with a wet fish." That thought brought the hint of a smile to her face, but there was no one there to see it.

And the holidays were approaching—Thanksgiving, and after that Christmas. Would anyone come out to see her? She certainly didn't have enough money to go back east, nor did she have any accrued vacation time. What would she do? What could she do? It was way too late, or early, to call either of her mothers, nor would she, at least not right now. Not when she'd burst into tears if she heard the sound of a familiar voice. No, she would e-mail them both tomorrow and convince them both to get with the times and learn the electronic intricacies of Skype.

And what about Jim Sawicki, Olympia's beloved friend, Father Jim. Laura smiled at the thought of Jim as she turned onto her side, tucked her right hand under her chin and wiggled herself into her going-to-sleep position. Her thoughts were no longer racing, and she felt herself relaxing into comfort of the mattress beneath her. In the short time she'd known Jim she'd fully accepted him as a member in good standing of her newly discovered extended family. She wondered what was he doing and where he was doing it. Before she'd left for California, he had performed her mother's marriage to Frederick. She knew he'd left the Roman Catholic Church and was currently going through the formal process of becoming a priest in the Episcopal Church. Such a good man, she thought, but a lonely one, I think.

This last thought remained incomplete as Laura finally drifted down into a dreamless sleep.

Robert Mosely had the tea ready and waiting in the sitting room when Margery came through the door of their cottage. Thomas the cat was curled in his accustomed place in front of the fire, waiting for his daily tablespoon of milk in his own saucer, if you please. It all looked and smelled and sounded so very ordinary and familiar, only it wasn't, and they both knew it.

"How was your day, love?" asked Robert.

"Always better when the Red Queen Attison isn't there, looking into things she shouldn't be. She was in a right stew over the meeting we cancelled. Then she said she had a doctor's appointment and left early. I had the rest of the afternoon to myself, so I stayed on and got things in order. Good thing, too, because we had a couple that was booked in for Sunday show up two days early. I got them sorted. "

"Did Celia say anything more about outside auditors before she left?"

"She didn't say much of anything after we sat and talked in the dining room other than she was having stomach problems and didn't feel well. Fancy that!" Margery touched the side of her nose with her index finger and winked at her husband.

"Might you happen to have an idea what all that might be about?"

"I might just," answered Margery.

Robert frowned and shook his head. "When you first told me about this plan of yours, you said there would be nothing to hurt or injure, just inconvenience. Have you gone and changed your mind?"

Margery smiled and changed the subject. "Have you given Thomas his milk then? Come on, cat. Who's a clever handsome boy?"

After Olympia and Frederick finished their tea and biscuits, they went out through the back door to get their cases. Before they left Olympia had been ruthless in their packing, adamantly limiting each of them to one manageable check-in case and one carry-on. Now all of her cajoling and haranguing was paying off. In minutes they were unpacked and settled in. As she looked around the room Olympia realized that she'd forgotten to ask anyone about internet connections and knew she would need to do that before long. She had promised to stay in e-mail contact with Jim and her children.

She checked her watch and noted that they had at least an hour before dinner would be served. Then, for no reason she could discern, she was suddenly overcome with longing and concern for her daughter.

Frederick picked up on it at once. "Is something wrong, my love?"

Olympia shook her head. "For no reason I can explain, I'm suddenly worried about my daughter."

"What brought that on?"

"I don't know. I'd call her, but I don't know if or where there's a phone I can use, and if my time calculations are right, she'll either be at work or asleep. No doubt I'm just being a worrywart, but the feeling is so strong. It could also just be a convoluted form of jet lag."

Frederick reached took both her hands in his. "We'll go downstairs and ask about the internet and a telephone, and if there isn't one here, we'll get in the car and drive until we can find either or both."

"I suppose we could go over and ask Margery Mosely. I saw her going into their cottage when we were getting our cases."

Frederick looked doubtful. "Let's see what we can find here first. We gave Laura and the boys my sister's telephone number and Jim's telephone number before we left in case anybody needed to reach us. Let's start by calling my sister and asking if anyone's called, and then we'll ... what the hell?"

He'd been interrupted by the muted sound of something metallic coming from the direction of the wardrobe.

"Olympia?"

She grinned sheepishly and said, "It's the clock."

"What clock? I didn't pack a clock. Did you get a travel alarm or something?"

"It's Miss Winslow's clock. We were on the way out the door when I grabbed it and stuffed it in my carry-on along with my computer."

"Bloody hell," said Frederick.

"Don't ask me why, because I can't tell you. I just knew I had to take it – or her, whatever, with me."

Frederick shook his head and chuckled. "You know what, my darling, I think it may well be a very good thing you did. Don't I always say that three heads are better than two? With Jim back in the States, I'm just as happy we have our dear Leanna here to advise us if we need it. Meanwhile, let's go prospecting for a phone and see if we can put your mind at ease. But before we do, take the clock out of the wardrobe and give the poor thing a breath of fresh air. Then you dust her off and set it on the nightstand between the beds. That way she can keep an eye on us."

"We might embarrass her."

"Hmmm, I hadn't thought of that."

"This is so bizarre," said Olympia. "If I read this in a book, I wouldn't believe it."

"If it works for us, does it matter what other people think?"

"Not in the slightest, my dear," said Olympia, carefully setting the clock down on the nightstand and giving it a reassuring little pat on the top of its smooth mahogany case. "Not in the slightest."

By eight in the evening they'd located the internet room, found a telephone and called Frederick's sister, Jenny Elder, and learned there were no messages from anyone. No news was definitely good news as far as Olympia was concerned, and she was ready to relax and join the ramblers gathered in the lounge for a glass of wine and some local color.

There were several people seated in the high-ceilinged room, all of whom looked up and smiled as she and Frederick opened the door and entered the room. When they heard her New England twang, they jiggled and jostled and beckoned them into the circle around the coal fire flickering in the grate. When all were resettled, they began introducing themselves. Jamie and Alice were from Perth in Scotland. John and Jean had come up from Kent. Maggie and Agnes were originally from Lancashire but now lived in a semi-detached in Gateshead and were still trying to make sense of the Geordie accent. This caused a ripple of laughter among all but Olympia. She turned a questioning eye to Frederick, who said he'd explain later.

The six had become fast friends years ago when they were all at university. Since then they gathered at The Moorlands once or twice a year to visit, reminisce and ramble together over and through the surrounding hills and dales.

"So you all have some history here," said an instantly alert Olympia.

"Aye, that we do," said Jamie.

"Ohhh, but it's not like it was when we first started coming here, is it, Jamie?" said his wife.

"Better or worse?" asked Frederick.

"Worse," offered Agnes. "It's been a slow decline. These places are impossible to heat and keep up. I think at one point they tried to give it to the National Trust, but even they didn't want it. I'd hate to see it close, because the location is perfect for all of us, and it's so beautiful here. But to be honest I don't see how they can keep it open for very much longer."

"Is it really that bad?" asked Olympia. "I can see it's a little run down at the edges, but isn't that part of the charm of these places, gently decaying elegance of another age that people really work hard to preserve?"

Jamie looked doubtful. "Aye, but there comes a point of no return, and if you ask me, I think that day might not be too far off."

Agnes held up her hands. "We're getting far too gloomy here. What will be, will be, and I don't think there's much any of us can do about it, so let's change the subject. Tell me, Olympia and Frederick, what brings you two here? Did you come to do some walking?"

Before Frederick could say anything Olympia smiled in the general direction of everyone and said, "I'm actually here to help out with a church leadership development conference that's being held here next week."

"And we got here early so we could do a little hiking," added Frederick. "Olympia really hasn't seen much of the un-touristy parts of England, so I thought this would be a perfect time and place to start."

"I was wondering if you might have some recommendations for us," said Olympia.

This produced a bit of shifting and digging into pockets, and then three of the six held out ordinance survey maps and guidebooks to Frederick and Olympia."

"I'd stick to the marked paths and roadways if you're a beginner. There's a lovely walk from here due west to the next town, and there's a lovely little pub, goes back to the fourteen hundreds. You can have lunch and a decent pint and still be back by dinnertime," said Agnes.

"And if you go west in the morning and east in the afternoon, you won't be looking into the sun, will you?" added Maggie.

"Good thinking," said Olympia.

"Should we tell Mrs. Mosely we won't be here for lunch?" asked Frederick.

Alice answered him. "I'd speak to Mrs. Darcie in the dining room. She'll sort it out for you. That Mosely woman is an odd one. She never has a good word for anyone except her husband and Mrs. Loring, the cook. She's been here for as long as we've been coming. Isn't that so, Jamie?"

"Some things get better with age, but not that one," added her husband.

"If she's such an old besom, I wonder why she's been allowed to stay on?" Olympia was the picture of innocent curiosity.

Alice responded. "She's good at what she does, is my guess. The office staff usually doesn't have too much contact with the guests. We only ever see her on weekends if the managing director isn't in."

Olympia cocked her head to one side. "Managing director?"

John from Kent responded. "That would be Celia Attison. She's new, only been here for six months or so. From what I hear they hired her to try and turn the place around, but I think she's flogging a dead horse. It's none of our concern really. I love coming here, but if it closes up shop, we'll just find someplace else, won't we, Jean?"

Olympia hid a yawn and nudged Frederick. "May we take these maps and things back to our room and look at them? We'll probably take your advice and just walk up to the next town and back, but I'd like to see what else is in the area."

This was greeted with a murmur of assents and goodnights and sleep-wells as Frederick and Olympia took their leave.

When the two were settled into their respective beds, he with a book and she about to open Miss Winslow's diary, Frederick asked, "So what are your initial impressions?"

"Of what?"

"This place."

"Too soon to tell," said Olympia.

November 12, 1862

We had our first snow today, just a feather dusting, here and gone by noon. Too many days have passed since I last wrote in these pages. My book ... yes I now have the courage to call it a book, consumes much of my time, and Jonathan takes up the rest. I have written to Aunt Louisa and asked if she will come and stay the winter with us, but I have not yet received her response. She is of an age when I would prefer she not be alone when the weather is bad, though I dare not say that in her hearing else I shall never hear the end of it. Little Jonathan adores her, and Christmas would be so much merrier with another adult in residence. I must ask Richard if he will join us for Christmas dinner—but listen to me, it is the middle of November, and Christmas is over six weeks hence. Louisa is right ... I am lonely.

More anon, LFW

Seven

The next morning Celia and Richard Attison were having a late breakfast in the sunny corner of their kitchen. Celia's stomach problems seemed to have subsided, and for the first time in several days she felt like eating. Her husband was celebrating her improved state of health by treating his wife to a full English breakfast of sausage, eggs, tomatoes, beans, mushrooms and toast to be washed down with huge mugs of strong tea.

"By the the way you are tucking into your breakfast, I'd say you are feeling better," said Richard.

"The doctor couldn't find anything physically wrong with me when I visited the surgery yesterday. He did ask if I was under any undue stress at home or perhaps at work. I confess I started laughing and then told him that other than my job was a living hell, why, nothing at all. Now that I'm home, and I don't have to go back for another whole day, I feel fine. Look at me, I'm eating like a horse."

"Am I mistaken, or does your stomach bother you only on those days when you are at work and not when you are here at home?"

Celia stopped eating and looked across the table at her husband. "Now that you mention it, yes. Not so much at the beginning of the week, but it seems to start up again on Tuesday or Wednesday, and then it keeps getting worse and worse until the weekend. I wonder why that is?"

"I think your doctor has it sussed. That job is making you sick. Why don't you just chuck it and leave? We can make it on my salary for a couple of months. I'd rather be pinching pennies for a while than have you stretched beyond yourself."

She put down her mug with a short sharp thump and said, "No! I was hired to turn that place around, and I'm not giving up, at least not until I've done everything I can to make a go of it. It's a beautiful place, you know that; it's got the whole history of the district in those stones. I think it's simply been mismanaged for too long—you know, the same people working there since the beginning of time. Policies and practices that worked in the forties and fifties simply don't work today. People who come to guest houses today are used to things working, toilets that flush and fridges that work and people who smile and make them feel welcome. The cook and the bookkeeper and the grounds manager have been there since the year dot and are totally unwilling to look at anything that means change. If I could do one thing that would make a difference to the survival of that place, it would be to get rid of the three of them."

Richard was taken aback by her vehemence. "Are they really that bad?"

Celia nodded grimly. "Not half. From what I can see Margery Mosely is the worst of the lot. She's an unhappy woman. You can see it in her face. Her husband is a good sort, and by God, can he fix things. I've never met the like of him. He knows the inside and outside of everything in the place, but he and the cook take their orders from her. Even though I'm supposed to be the managing director, nothing I say gets done unless she gives it the okay. Not so I notice it, mind you, but over the years she's secured her position in the pecking order, and nothing short of radical surgery is going to unseat her."

Richard pushed away his plate and put his elbows on the table. "Have you taken this up with the board? They hired you, didn't they? Do they know what's going on?"

"Not directly. Not yet, anyway. I've made some suggestions about new blood, fresh ideas and becoming more technically savvy in terms of communication and record-keeping, but when I do, all they do is look at the ceiling and hum and haw and eventually change the subject. Old loyalties run deep, and the Moselys have been here from the beginning. It's not so much about getting rid of them as it is trimming the waste and introducing some new and more efficient ideas, and she's dead set against anything that isn't her idea."

"So it really is an impossible task then?"

"I didn't say that."

"But it's making you sick, or something there is making you sick."

Celia looked down. She'd been bested. The man was right, and she knew he was, but she still wasn't ready to give up. "Look, Richard, you are going to be there all next week. They expect you to be involved in your conference, but you can certainly keep your eyes and ears open and tell me what you see and hear. What about this Olympia Brown person? I've only heard you talk about her, but clearly you think enough of her to ask her to come and do one of the big workshops for you. Don't say anything to her beforehand, but afterward you might ask her what she thinks about the operation from the perspective of a guest of the establishment."

Now it was Richard's turn to look away, and then he looked back with a smile. "Funny you should say that. I had that very thought myself. Some of these country folk still think of the Yanks as upstart colonists and will pay them little heed. They might be a little less guarded in their conversations."

"Well, then, there's a case to be made for having a quick word with her when she gets here on Sunday afternoon."

Richard paused and lined up his knife and spoon with the edge of the table mat before responding. "It's your call, Celia, but I think that's a good idea. I haven't seen her since my semester at Harvard Divinity School, and that was a good eight or nine years ago. People don't change. She's as bright as a new penny and clever with it. You'll be at The Moorlands on Sunday to check people in and help them find their rooms. Once

Olympia and her husband are settled in, let's see if we find a time before supper for a quick cup of tea away from the others. Have a talk with her, and see how she strikes you. Then, if you feel you want to, tell her what's going on, or perhaps what you think is going on."

Celia nodded sadly. "That's just it. Is there something intentional going on to discredit me and make me look incompetent, or am I getting paranoid?" She paused and rubbed at her chin. "While I'm inclined to think there is something deliberate, the question is why? Is it only resistance to change? I think they know that if we don't take a deep hard look at what's left of the endowment and how the finances are being managed, we don't have a future, but at the same time they can't, or won't, look beyond the noses on their collective faces. If the place folds, no one will have a job." She shook her head in frustration. "It is so short sighted. What does anyone have to gain if the place goes under?"

"Sounds like a case of mass denial to me. You know, if I can't see or won't look at the problem, then there is no problem," said Richard.

"Oh, there's a problem, all right," said Celia.

"And are you convinced you are the only person in England with the solution to that problem?"

"At one point I thought I was, Richard, but I'm not going to know anything until I get a chance to look into the accounting system closely with an expert. I do know we're leaking money from somewhere; that's why I'm calling for an audit. Nonprofits and charitable institutions are not expected to lose money. They need to be self-sustaining so they can continue to do their work and support the mission of the organization. That's not happening at The Moorlands."

"Four heads are better than two, Celia. Let's hold off until we talk to Olympia and Frederick."

"Frederick?"

"He's Olympia's new husband. They were married a couple of weeks ago. He's a Geordie."

Celia chuckled. "I hope I'll be able to understand him. I wonder how they met."

"I suspect if you ask, they'll tell you. I don't know the story myself, so I'll be interested to hear."

"So that's two things to talk about over our tea," said Celia.

"At the very least," said Richard.

After a full English breakfast of their own, Frederick and Olympia set off walking in the direction of the next village. They took with them a couple of granola bars, two large bottles of water and one of the maps Frederick had saved from the night before. The midmorning November light was pale and clear, and the country air was cool. Olympia could smell fresh earth and dried grass and occasionally the slightly acrid scent of coal smoke. There had been some talk of showers later in the day, but the two planned to be back long before midafternoon, when they were predicted to occur. They had agreed they would not speak of anything relating to the suspected trouble at the retreat center and instead give themselves over completely to the beauty of the day, the joy they found in one another and the expanse of Yorkshire moorland unfolding before them. Frederick was completely in his element. He was on his home turf, his beloved England. Even his accent had become stronger over the last few days.

Olympia, however, was not quite so enchanted. Breathtakingly beautiful as it was, within the first hour of slow but steady up and down hill walking, she was already wondering what in hell she had signed on to? She was determined not to pant or sweat but was reconsidering the resolution. Where was that next village that looked so close on the map, and for that matter, where the hell were they?

"Are we there yet?" said Olympia.

"Getting winded, are we?"

"Not at all. I just wondered how far it is from point A to point B. The map wasn't all that clear." To prove her point she squared her shoulders and deliberately stepped up her pace.

Frederick looked thoughtful. "One of the men last night said it was about a two-hour walk. Perhaps we should sit down and rest for a few minutes and have another look at the map."

Olympia realized with some dread that she'd entrusted the map, and therefore their route, to a man with no inborn sense of direction. The two stopped and leaned against a moss-flecked stone wall. Frederick pulled out the map and one of the water bottles, which they shared. Then he unfolded the map, turning it this way and that in an obvious attempt to make sense of it.

"Bugger!" he said.

"Wrong direction?" asked Olympia with not a little trepidation.

"Wrong map," said Frederick.

In a little room off the kitchen the cook, Mrs. Loring, and Margery Mosely were having a second cup of tea and a hushed conversation.

"She'll no doubt be here tomorrow afternoon when the new group arrives. She usually does. Her Royal Highness insists on greeting them all herself."

"So what should I be doing in the meanwhile?"

"Nothing straight away. Let her get the new lot settled in. You feed them supper and fill them up with your famous sticky toffee pudding. That way we'll have them full and happy, and all will be right with the world."

"Then what?"

"Things happen, don't they?"

Margery drank down the last of her tea and began collecting her things.

"I'll just rinse out this cup and leave it on the drainboard."

"Leave it in the sink. The girls will still be doing the lunch dishes. Let them earn their keep for once."

Margery was heading back to her office when Olympia and Frederick came staggering in, soaked and bedraggled, through the front door.

"Well, you two are a sight," said Margery.

"We got ourselves rather lost," said Frederick.

"More like we took the wrong map," growled Olympia as sweetly as she could.

"Ohhhh, there's a bit of bad luck." Margery tsk-ed a few times and shook her head.

"Then it started to rain, and we didn't have a brolly." Frederick was looking and sounding more piteous by the minute.

"It was predicted; you should have taken one. We always keep extra brollies and wooly jumpers for the guests."

"What, and plan ahead? Surely you jest, Mrs. Mosely. Clearly, you don't know my husband very well."

"Olympia!"

"Sorry, darling. I need a hot shower and some dry clothes right this minute." Olympia stalked off in the direction of her room, leaving Frederick dripping on the floor and Mrs. Mosely tight-lipped.

"Americans," said Frederick, desperately trying to save face. "They've got no sense of adventure."

"Aye," said Margery Mosely.

Eight

On Sunday midday, as planned, Celia and Richard drove from their home to The Moorlands. She, being the faster driver of the two, arrived first, and he pulled in shortly after in his own car. He planned to stay the week at The Moorlands, and she needed to go back and forth to see to the dog and the plants. Once they learned that Olympia and Frederick had already been checked in, the two went and found them finishing their lunch in the dining room.

The Attisons were full of apologies for not coming in earlier, but Olympia firmly assured them it was her specific request that their personal time not be disturbed. She went on to say that she and Frederick needed to reset their body clocks to UK time and have a little opportunity to ramble around on their own. Mercifully, she left out the part about their getting lost, soaked and frozen. Some things are better left unsaid, and it was still a very tender subject.

Frederick pulled out a chair and invited them to join them at the table, but Celia quickly waved him off. She looked down at her watch.

"The others won't be here for at least an hour, so why don't you both come and join me in my office for some tea and biscuits? That way the ladies can clear up the dining room, and we won't be in their way."

"What a good idea. You all go on ahead. I'll clear our things off the table and catch you up in two shakes," said Frederick.

"Do you know where my office is?" asked Celia.

"I do. That woman, Mrs. Mosely, took us in there when we arrived on Friday. She wrote us into the book and then showed us to our room. Very efficient."

"She's all of that," said Celia.

By the time Frederick walked into Celia's office, the others were well into their tea and onto their second biscuit.

"What took you so long? I thought you were coming right behind us."

"I decided to stay and finish my pudding and have a quick look at the crossword."

"That's fine; we were just catching each other up."

"It seems a long time, and at the same time it seems like yesterday that we last saw each other," said Richard.

Olympia smiled fondly in his direction. "That's the way it is with good friends. We've gone our separate ways over these several years, but it's clear the common ground is still there. But listen to me, there's time for catching up later. I suppose you want to go over the so-called operating instructions for the conference before the others get here, do you not?"

Celia shook her head. "Actually, I have something considerably less official than that I want to talk about. Has Richard said anything to you about what may or may not be happening here?"

Richard's eyebrows joined forces in the middle of his face, and Olympia took the cue. She didn't want to tell an outright lie, but she could speak the truth very carefully.

"When he first called me, Richard did say there were some, er, issues here at The Moorlands that could be of some future concern. Because of that he said we would be keeping a very tight hold on the conference budget, but it shouldn't really affect the quality of our program as long as I didn't expect to get paid. Did I miss anything, Richard?"

Back to you, brother, she thought.

"That's pretty much it, Olympia. The Moorlands, like most charitable organizations, is suffering financially, but then so is just about everything in this current economy."

Then Celia held up her hand. "There is more, and to be honest I wasn't sure how much I wanted to tell you or anyone other than Richard. But hearing you two talk just now, and hearing what's happened in some of your churches, it's possible you might be able to give us some insight that someone on the inside of the operation might not be able to offer."

Olympia cocked her head to one side. "I can try, Celia, but it would help if you could tell me a little more of what I should be looking for."

Celia leaned forward in her chair and lowered her voice. "Moorlands is having financial problems, huge ones, but I've come to think the issue is not about balancing the budget. We've had to spend down some of the endowment, but lots of places are forced to do that. No, I think it's deeper and wider than cash flow. We get enough people using The Moorlands for conferences, retreats and even weddings to make a go of it, and yet we're going under. It's clear to me we're leaking money from somewhere, and I don't think it's just started. I think it has been going on for some time."

"Not that you've asked me," said Frederick, "but it sounds to me like you need to take a good look at the books, perhaps call in an outside auditor. That's what I'd do."

"That's exactly what I suggested to the board."

"What did they say?" asked Olympia.

"A lot of gasps and 'can't be' and 'surely not' and even one 'surely you are not accusing one of us?' But after a long dark silence, the idea was tabled with suggestions that perhaps they ought to form a committee, and yes, someday they would look into it, but certainly not now."

"Then what?"

"Then everything I did or said became suspect. They thought I had taken against all of them, and then things started happening."

"Tell them what kinds of things," prompted her husband.

Celia frowned. "This is where it becomes unclear. Little things: drains clogging, burnt food, rooms not made up when they were supposed to be. Nothing that in and of itself would have been anything more than a minor inconvenience, but collectively they mount up. It's starting to make me look incompetent, and it's damaging the reputation of The Moorlands."

Olympia nodded but said nothing. She'd seen this kind of thing before. It was the worst kind of passive aggression. Never do anything overt, but just let everything slow down and slide away until it's beyond repair, and then walk away from the rubble, claiming not to have any idea how it happened.

"It's amazing what people will say when they think you're part of the wallpaper," said Frederick.

"Whatever do you mean?" asked Richard.

"Just that. I'm of no account. I'm not a minister, and I'm not registered for the conference. I'm not even foreign and therefore totally unworthy of note. Just another bloke from the countryside with no pedigree, here for a free week while the wife is giving a workshop. I might as well have been a milk jug for all the heed they paid to me."

"What are you saying, Frederick?"

"I'm saying that because they took absolutely no notice of me when I was finishing my lunch, they carried on as though I wasn't there. The Mosely woman and the cook were having a bit of a natter in the back room off the kitchen. I couldn't make out the words, but whatever it was, it sounded serious."

"How could you tell?" asked Celia.

"One can easily tell if a conversation is serious or not, no laughter, hushed and guarded low tones. Mosely had a scowl a foot wide on her when she came into the dining room. She walked right by me without a glance."

Celia looked annoyed. "I'll have to speak to her about that. All the staff, from the top to the bottom, are supposed to make the guests here feel comfortable and welcome at all times."

"Actually, Celia, if it's all the same to you I'd rather you said nothing and let them carry on as they will. If they think I'm not worthy of notice, then they won't be guarded in my presence. They're all on their best behavior when any of you lot are in the room."

"I think I see what you're getting at," said Richard.

Celia pointed to the clock on the wall and then turned to Olympia. "We don't have much time before people will be starting to arrive. I wonder if you and Frederick would simply spend the week watching and listening. I'll admit the whole thing has made me so anxious I'm having stomach problems. Then I ask myself if I'm imagining things, and it's just that I got off on the wrong foot when I first arrived, and they are not about to let me forget it." She paused. "But I don't know which."

Olympia raised her hand like a school girl. "Maybe we could get together again later in the week and compare notes?"

"I'd love to be proven wrong," said Celia.

Olympia put a reassuring hand on her arm. "I'll do my best."

Celia smiled and stood up. "It's time we went out and started meeting and greeting the incoming guests."

"Let battle commence," said Frederick.

"This is just a matter of inquiry, my dear, not a holy war."

"I'm not so sure about that."

By late in the afternoon on Sunday the last two conferees, Rosemary Lewis and Steve Warner, had been duly registered and shown up to their rooms. They cheerily apologized to all and sundry for being so slow in getting there, claiming unfamiliar roads and unclear local maps. Olympia nodded sympathetically but wisely held her own counsel. Her mother had always said discretion was the better part of valor. In this case, her discretion was keeping charitably quiet, not pouring salt in a still fresh wound. Getting lost was not a laughing matter.

With some free time remaining until dinner, a few of them elected to go out and explore the one-lane village of Little Humblesby. The others went in search of a cup of tea and a comfortable chair where they could unwind and wait for the dinner bell.

Once it sounded, Richard and Celia Attison and Olympia and Frederick joined the cluster of hungry souls gathered at the door of the dining room. Olympia was standing off to the side, listening to the chatter and watching the body language. They were an interesting lot. Most were parish ministers, but two were lay leaders of small parishes which could not afford to retain a proper minister. Usually congregations like this managed to hold themselves together by sharing common vision along with a dogged determination to keep going in an increasingly secular world.

It's the same the whole world over, she thought, watching them all and catching fragments of their conversations. So many people are looking for something to hold onto and believe in that gives meaning to their lives. The difficulty so often comes in trying to agree on how to conduct the search and, even more basic than that, what is the nature of the search itself.

"I suppose the conversation has to begin with what we are looking for."

"What was that?" asked Frederick.

Olympia shook her head and held up her hand. "Sorry, love, I guess I was thinking out loud. Oh, look, they've opened the door, and I smell food." She lifted her head and sniffed appreciatively. "M-m-m-m."

The conferees moved into the dining room and made their way to the two round tables that were set up for them. They were the only guests in residence and thus had the whole place to themselves. The room was institutionally cheerful with pale yellow walls, white oft-mended cloths on the tables and a basket of artificial flowers in the middle of each one. The window wall had no curtains, only pull shades to keep out the sun when needed. It was the view that made this room inviting and wonderful. The windows opened out onto the moorlands, a vast undulating sweep of gorse and sheep-sprinkled hillsides and valleys. Olympia moved quickly to a seat where she could look out over all this and unfolded her napkin in her lap.

After the serving bowls and platters were set in place on the tables, Rosemary Lewis was the first to introduce herself. She said she was a social worker by profession and the lay leader of a small congregation in The Potteries. When they needed a minister for a wedding or a funeral, Richard Attison did the honors.

"Potteries? That's one I haven't heard of," said Olympia.

"Oh, that's the local name. Many of the major pottery and porcelain factories were located in Staffordshire and around Stoke. Huge natural clay deposits and such in the area. No doubt you've heard of Josiah Wedgewood," she said with an authoritative smile.

"I have indeed," said Olympia.

"He was an early benefactor of our chapel," said Rosemary.

"You do like to bring that up, don't you? I guess it's my turn. I'm Gillian Steele, and I'm a parish minister in a village that's east of here near Skipton. They are a lovely group of people, but we need some new ideas. I've come for that reason and to be with other ministers for a while. It gets lonely out there sometimes."

Olympia nodded sympathetically. She knew exactly what Gillian meant, but before she could speak to the subject the woman sitting to Olympia's left introduced herself.

"I'm Janet Lofton, and I think I'm the junior member here. I'm thinking about taking an advanced degree, but every time I mention it my congregation gives me ten more reasons why I shouldn't, and I stay on. So like you, Gillian, I need some new ideas and maybe some energy to go along with it."

The man sitting next to Rosemary was next. "I'm Stephen Warner, and I serve part time in a chapel outside of Manchester. I have a wife, a son and two cats, and I'd love to visit the States some time."

I'll put him on file later, thought Olympia. He gets extra points for cats and for wanting to come to the States. Maybe they could do a pulpit swap sometime. Then she remembered she didn't exactly have a pulpit she could swap. Never mind! She would have a conversation with him sometime in the coming week.

Olympia wished she could be at both tables so she could have a sense of who they all were before they got started later that evening. She could hear the people at the next table doing the same thing. Some were more assertive in tone and manner and others less so, but the ritual of introducing themselves was well underway. They were a group of twelve—ten really if you didn't count Frederick and Celia. But these twelve would likely be having meals and tea and talking breaks together over the next six days. It wasn't much time.

Suddenly the task before her began to feel overwhelming. Could she really be an effective workshop leader in the conference and at the same time keep an ear to the wall of The Moorlands? Then she remembered the offer Frederick had made on the plane. Of course! He might be the man who took the wrong map on their walk yesterday. He might be the man who got them hopelessly lost and then soaked to the skin when the predicted showers caught them a mile from home. But he was also the man who uncharacteristically flagged down a passing motorist and asked for a lift back to The Moorlands. Yes, Frederick would be the secret ingredient in her improper little mission.

"Yup, that'll work all right."

"What was that?" asked Frederick.

"Talking to myself again, I guess."

"And are you going to let your husband in on your little secret?"

"In due time, she said, and then she sneezed.

"Oh, dear, you're not catching cold are you?" He looked concerned.

Olympia muttered under her breath, "And for your health and safety, my marvelous and meandering English darling, I hope the hell I'm not."

"Say again?"

"Ask me in the morning, Frederick. Meanwhile, what is this I see before me?"

Annette Darcie, the dining room hostess and supervisor had just placed a plate of something dark and shining and steaming with caramel and nuts before her. The smell alone was intoxicating.

"Ahhhhhh," sighed Stephen Warner, "sticky toffee pudding with pouring cream. Don't wake me now. I think I've just died and gone to heaven."

"I believe a chorus of 'yums' just went 'round the table," said Frederick, looking just as blissful as the rest of them and spooning up a mouthful out of the mound of calories set before him.

Olympia hesitated. "Sticky toffee pudding? It certainly smells delicious, but it doesn't look like pudding. It's a piece of cake with some sauce on it. Pudding is soft and gooey."

Richard Attison called over from the next table. "Try it, Olympia. It's England's secret and most potent weapon. We could win wars with this stuff, but we like it too much to give any away."

Just as Olympia was about to enjoy her first decadent spoonful, an ashen-faced Celia Attison leapt out of her chair, knocked over her water glass and bolted out of the room with her husband running after her.

Later that evening when they were gathered in the sitting room, Richard Attison explained that his wife sent apologies for disturbing their dinner. She had a sudden recurrence of a rather nasty tummy-bug and prudently decided to go home.

"It's been bothering her for some time, but her doctor assured her just last week that it was nothing to worry about. She probably tried to come back to work too soon."

This was received with knowing nods and murmurs and a collective sigh of relief.

"Right. With that out of the way, let us begin our introductions. I know you did some of this around the table at dinner, but not everybody met everyone else, so let's do a quick round-up, and you can fill in the spaces over the week."

Vaughn Weller cleared his throat and introduced himself, saying he was from the West Country, where he was the lay leader of a small congregation in the village of Gotton, and his interest was really church management, as well as leadership. He in turn was followed by a minister who stood up and introduced himself as Peter Wamsley. "I'm between churches at the moment. I've just completed a long tenure with a congregation in the south, and I'm taking a year off and pursuing some courses at Manchester College before I start looking again. Actually, I'm not sure whether I'll stay in Parish ministry. I was delighted to learn that Reverend Brown was going to be in attendance, because if we can find the time, I'd like to hear about opportunities for ministry in the States. I'm thinking about new directions."

Several others in the room nodded in agreement, and Richard Attison picked up on it at once.

"Interesting you should say that, Peter. Although Olympia and I haven't' exactly planned out our agenda hour by hour, I think it is safe to say we can certainly spend some time hearing about what's happening in sister churches across the pond. What say, Madame Reverend?"

Olympia, who had been more of an observer than a participant thus far, suddenly sat up to attention. "I'd be more than delighted. Actually, I'm very interested in what's happening here, so I think a good exchange of ideas on principles and practices might be just the thing. Why don't we try and work that into the schedule?"

"Hopes and pipedreams might be a more accurate title, but whatever we call it, I think I can safely say we would all be interested. Now then, is there anyone we haven't heard from?"

An attractive, slender woman waved from her spot at the outer of the edge of the circle.

"Yes to everything you've said so far. I'm Catherine Collins, and I'm a hospice chaplain. I help out a couple of times a year at a tiny chapel near Alnwick in Northumberland. The reason I signed up for this was so I could be with colleagues and hear what we all are doing in the towns and villages. This can be a very lonely business."

Stephen Warner nodded sympathetically. "I'll say. With fewer and fewer people going to church at all, and those that still do growing older and more frail, it does make you wonder if there's a future for any of us."

"Well, that's why we're here isn't it?" Rosemary Lewis made a sweeping gesture that embraced them all. "The Moorlands is a religious retreat and conference center. Somebody cared enough about the role of organized religion in England to fund and establish this place. It's still here, and we're here right now, so somebody besides us thinks we have a future."

Richard Attison flicked a quick glance at Olympia and just as quickly turned back toward the group and spoke in a more serious and guarded voice.

"It's no secret that The Moorlands is struggling financially, but so is every charitable organization in the UK. They'll find a way to survive, or they won't, and there's not much we can do to affect it one way or the other. It's not like we have vast reserves in our own churches that we can draw upon to lend assistance."

This produced a round of low chuckles and sympathetic head nodding as Richard continued.

"Our job this week is to work together, to share ideas and to be truly present to one another. Who knows? Even though it's not on our agenda, maybe among all of us we may even come up with some ideas that might be of use to The Moorlands."

"Here, here," said Vaughn, raising an imaginary glass.

"Don't quit your day job," muttered Olympia.

"What was that, love?" asked Frederick.

"I said it's going to be an interesting week."

"No, you didn't."

"Well, that's what I meant," she said, and then she sneezed.

"Hot whiskey and lemon for you, Missus," said Frederick.

"Hold the lemon," said Olympia.

Nine

November 22, 1862

Pale sun today and a light wind, but not too cold. I was overjoyed to receive a letter from Aunt Louisa telling me she will come and stay the winter. Her arrival date depends on how quickly she can pack her things and close up the house in Cambridge. I shall ask Richard if he will collect her at the train station and bring her here. Later in the day I received a second letter from a Boston lawyer saying that I was to expect delivery of a parcel within the week. I recognized the name; he was the conduit of information and messages from Jonathan's late father. Whatever can this be? I am disquieted by too many memories.

More anon, LFW

Olympia closed the diary, set it on the table between their beds and groaned. She felt like death warmed over, a descriptive phrase her mother had used when she was really sick. Her sneezes of the night before had been the early warning signs of the cold from hell. I need this like I need a hole in the head, she grumbled to herself. The whiskey and lemon—Frederick had insisted upon the lemon—had done little, if anything, to help the situation. Her nose was running, her head was pounding, she was three thousand miles from home in a strange bed with no cats to comfort her, she had blisters on both heels, and she was furious. She was annoyed with herself for catching cold. She was mad at Frederick for getting her soaked and chilled, not to mention getting them lost on that seemingly endless and circuitous walk. She growled at the memory.

Most of all she was in no mood to get up and spend the day talking and being nice to a group of people she didn't know. This was not like her, and she knew it; but she felt awful, and all the tea, lemon, whiskey and even wine, ice cream and chocolate were not going to make her feel any better at this stage. She knew the drill: lots of water, vitamin C, rest when she could and try not to snap at perfectly nice people who would keep asking if she was feeling any better.

"Would you like me to bring you a cup of tea, my love?" Frederick, still in his pajamas, was standing beside her bed with a towel over his arm and his toothbrush in hand. He looked like a tousled head waiter.

Olympia snuffled and nodded gratefully.

"Let me have a wash, and I'll get right to it. What time do things begin for you this morning?"

"Not until nine-thirty."

"You mean half-nine."

Olympia groaned. "I don't know what I mean any more. I feel like I have to get better to die!"

He reached down and stroked her cheek with the back of his index finger. "I'll be back in two shakes. Do you think you can hang on until then?"

Olympia nodded, wiggled herself back down under the duvet and closed her eyes.

In the private room off the kitchen Margery and the cook, one of her confidantes, were in the midst of an intense conversation.

"Did you serve our dear managing director anything other than what was on the menu? I'm told she became violently ill and left early."

The cook shook her head and raised her right hand. "Go get a Bible if you want to, Margery. With God as my witness, I didn't do anything. I have no idea what set her off. All I know is that she was eating her supper and was suddenly taken ill. Your guess is as good as mine."

"Her husband just came in and told me she's poorly and won't be in today. That means I get to do her job and mine." She paused and peered at the cook over her spectacles. "But now that I think about it, there could be worse misfortunes at sea."

"Whatever do you mean by that, Margery Mosely?"

"I mean while that mouse is away, this cat will play."

"Play at what?" asked the cook.

Margery paused as a slow and unpleasant smile began to spread across her face. "Although I didn't realize it until this very minute, a day without Celia Attison in attendance is exactly what I need."

Once Olympia and the others were shut away in the conference room, Frederick decided to have a little meander about the grounds. In truth, there wasn't a lot to see. Much of the original estate had been let out as grazing land to local sheep farmers. This made walking in the fields a bit of a hazard and likely not to be of much interest. As he slowly walked around the outside of the main house, he found a fenced-in formal flower garden on the western wall which, upon closer examination, proved to be a memory garden. There were benches here and there, some with memorial plaques, positioned around an open central area. At the far end he saw a vine-covered trellis offering an attractive focal spot where a minister might perform an outdoor wedding or christening.

From there he walked around to the back and to the south side and found the remains of a fairly substantial kitchen garden. He could see dried tomato and bean stalks, some wilted rhubarb leaves and some still-green clusters of herbs. He recognized parsley, dill, rosemary and great bunches of past-season lavender. Frederick leaned over and broke off a sprig of parsley, put it in his mouth and began to chew. The bright clean flavor reminded him of his mother's kitchen garden, always full of new seeds and good intentions when she planted it every spring and then sadly neglected and choked with weeds by mid-July. It was the same every year, an endearing family tradition; but with her death the sweet-sad humor of it all was gone forever. Now the smell and taste of the fresh parsley evoked a memory that was as sharp and clear as his mother's tongue, and despite his efforts to blink them back, tears pooled in his eyes behind his glasses.

"Morning."

Frederick was startled out of his reverie by a large man dressed in worn overalls and dusty wellingtons, holding out a large work-roughened hand.

"I'm Robert Mosely, fixer of all things bent and broken and lord and master of the toolshed. My wife Margery is the bookkeeper here, and I'm the caretaker of the house and grounds. She does the inside, and I do the outside." He paused and looked down. "And this 'ere is Thomas, protector of the realm."

Frederick looked down to see a sleek orange tomcat at his feet.

The big man inclined his head toward the building. "You with that lot in there?" He had a round, apple cheeked Yorkshire face and a wide-open grin.

Frederick shook his head. "Yes and no. My wife is part of the conference. I came along for a bit of a holiday. I brought some books, and I usually do the daily crossword, but who wants to stay indoors when the sun is shining?"

"Aye, not much of it these days. Do you keep a garden at home?"

Frederick fell into step beside him. "A little one, not as big as this. I grow pretty much the same things, but the summer is longer where I live, so I can usually get a few winter vegetables and potatoes, as well."

"Where d'ye live, then?"

"I live in the States now, but I grew up in the northeast … in canny Gateshead, man."

"Well, then you're either a long way from home, or you're not far from home at all. Which is it?"

Frederick pursed his lips. "I'm not sure. Probably a little bit of both. But this week I'm letting the wife do the work and having a few days to myself.

"Aye, the wives do like to keep us busy, don't they?" Mosely chuckled at his little joke. "It's not like I don't have enough to do on my own around this place. Every time I turn around, something falls off or breaks down, and while I'm working on that she comes and tells me about something I've missed."

"It's a lot to keep up, but surely they don't expect you to do it all by yourself, do they?"

"I've got old Bud Loring, he's cook's husband, but he's getting on. He can't do as much as he used to. He works mostly in the garden. Used to be I could fettle anything on the place, but it's all so much more complicated now. And don't even speak to me about computers." He snorted. "Margery, that's my wife, she's the brainy one. When they came out, first thing she did was take a course on how to use them. Always an eye to the main chance, that one. She's really kept up with the times. Not me. Give me a spade and some compost or a spanner and bit of copper tubing, and I'm happy. But listen to me. I'm talking your ears off. You must have things you need to be doing."

Frederick paused, held out his hand and said, "It's good to meet you, Robert Mosely, and to be back in England. I didn't realize how much I missed it." Then a quick smile brightened his face. "Say, if ever you need a hand around here, and you just said you did, do say the word."

"I might just do that," said Mosely, nodding in Frederick's direction.

"I'll hold you to it. In fact, I'd welcome it. Don't you breathe a word of it, but I can get a little restless while herself is in there brandishing her wisdom."

Mosely smiled. "If you really do mean it, and you have a mind to, there's a gate that needs a new hinge, and I could use an extra set of hands setting it right."

"Tell me when," said Frederick, fractionally puffing out his chest.

Mosely consulted his watch, pulled at his chin and said, "How about right after elevenses? With two of us on it, we can have it done before lunch. It's not a big job, just fiddly."

"I think it's just what the doctor ordered."

"How so?" asked a curious Mosely.

"If I were to be totally honest, I'd have to tell you that I wasn't entirely pleased with the idea of spending a whole week sitting alone inside with my books and my crosswords. A man needs to keep busy, and I like to be out in the fresh air."

"Aye," said Mosely, "I know what y'mean."

Frederick waved him off and started toward the back entrance. There was the morning taken care of. Later, with a little bit of luck and perhaps a word or two of advice from Mosely, he might have a plan for the afternoon, as well. If he weren't such a modest man, Frederick might be pleased with himself, but the husband of Olympia Brown knew more than most not to tempt fate. He'd learned long ago that most roads are not straight, and even the best and most carefully laid plans of mice and men need constant revision. He turned and watched Robert Mosely, with Thomas the cat at his heels, walk slowly and deliberately towards his cottage.

I do think something might be going on here, he thought, but what is it? He could sense it in the furtive mutterings of the household staff and see it in their obvious resentment of management. He'd learned from their evening with the ramblers and again the next day from Celia Attison that the place had a noble history but was now in financial trouble. He also knew

Margaret Mosely had no use whatsoever for Celia Attison. She'd made that clear the minute they arrived. But what about Robert Mosely? He seemed to be a good sort. Where did he fit into the mix, or did he fit into the mix at all? I'll know soon enough, he told himself. People often chat about this and that when they work together. Frederick smiled, but the smile quickly became a thoughtful frown. Today was Monday, and he and Olympia were scheduled to leave on the Friday. It didn't give them much time.

Inside the great stone building, secure in the conference meeting room, Richard Attison was leading a general discussion on the need and direction for greater trained lay leadership in small congregations. Olympia was looking on, huddled by the fireplace. She was wrapped in two borrowed sweaters, nursing a cup of tea and cradling a box of tissues in her lap. She was not a pretty sight, and she knew it. Occasionally, by way of token participation, she would croak something from her corner of the room, but for the most part she remained a most miserable observer, but an observer nonetheless. On the best of days Olympia Brown didn't miss much, and as awful as she felt at present, her evident misery gave her the opportunity to watch and wait in a way that might not have been offered to her had she felt more human. It was decidedly a mixed blessing, and typically, she chose the positive.

The discussion itself was pretty general and not particularly enlightening or fruitful, but Olympia knew that first meetings of any conference rarely are. People, even ministers, in a new situation tend to be cautious. She heard the usual topics of church governance come to the surface: too few people doing most of the work, the need for a collective vision and mission, the ever-present lack of money, dwindling attendance and the need to attract young families with children. They were familiar themes in her ringing ears, and she was beginning to drift off.

She came to attention with a start when the talk turned to the idea of having church and family weekend conferences at The Moorlands. She heard Richard Attison's voice take on a more serious tone.

"I wish I could say that church and family events here would be an option for us to explore, but to be honest, I have to say that I'm not at all certain how much longer The Moorlands will remain open for business." He paused and looked around the room before continuing. "This, of course, is confidential and must stay within the walls of this room. As you all know, my wife Celia is the managing director here, and it is enough to say she is gravely concerned about the future of this place. She's doing her best to save it, but the truth is the problem may be well beyond anyone's ability to turn around."

This was met with general sighs and mutterings of surprise and disappointment, which were promptly interrupted by the rattling and tinkling sound of the tea cart approaching the door of the conference room.

"Ahhhh, saved by the bell. It's time for elevenses." Richard Attison held a warning finger up to his lips and then turned and opened the door for a cheery Annette Darcie.

"Tea's up," she called.

Ten

Celia Attison was feeling better. The violent lower intestinal distress of the night before had stopped but not before she noticed blood in the toilet bowl. Now she was trying to decide whether to ring up her doctor. But hadn't he said the condition was probably stress related? And hadn't she just gone into work yesterday to start up a new conference? Any new group of guests made for stress until they were all sorted and settled into their rooms. There was no doubt that her job was affecting her, but all jobs involved some kind of stress, didn't they?

She started to reach for the phone beside her bed, and then she changed her mind. Richard can handle the group, and Mrs. Moseley can mind the office. I'll stay home and rest, drink plenty of fluids and see how I feel this evening. Celia knew that staying hydrated was critical. She'd not been able to keep much in or down for the last twenty hours, and she was weak and shaky. That's it, she reasoned with herself—rest, lots of liquids, boiled milk and rice when it will stay down and sleep when she could. She'd go back tomorrow. Really, when she thought about it, Richard was doing all the work—he and that friend of his, Olympia Brown. She smiled. Her first impression of Olympia had been most positive. Maybe things were looking better. Maybe there really was a way forward.

She rolled over in bed and noticed her laptop blinking at her, and she remembered the e-mail from the chartered accountant that in her distress she'd neglected to answer. More stress! No, sleep first, she told herself. The computer isn't going anywhere. Then a cup of ginger tea and a cream cracker. If that stayed down, she'd see about responding to the e-mail.

Frederick enjoyed his elevenses with the staff in the dining room and then followed Robert Mosely and Thomas outside and around to the back to the gate that needed mending. Methodical man that he was, Robert had already set out the tools and the new hinge. The two men, refreshed and emboldened by their tea and biscuits, were now ready to take on, if not the entire world, then at least the uncooperative gate.

He was feeling cheery. Robert Mosely was an amiable chap, and Frederick was looking forward to making himself useful out in the fresh air. It was fairly mild for November, and before long he took off his jacket and hung it on the fence post. Robert was explaining what needed doing. The old hinges had to be removed and the wood beneath it smoothed and checked for wood rot. If all was satisfactory, they could attach the new ones onto the gate. Then one man would hold it in place, and the other would screw the whole thing into place on the post.

Although Frederick had never actually replaced a gate hinge before, the task was straightforward, and he understood at once what needed doing. Before long the two men were working in tandem as though they'd been doing it for years. He understood his role, and it was to fetch things when needed and do as directed when instructed. He handed Mosely the tools as he asked for them, swept away wood shavings and picked up splinters as required, all the time chatting about this and that, the weather, the view, the foxes that lived nearby and what a lovely old place this must have been in its heyday.

Frederick was careful to keep the conversation light and innocuous. They complained agreeably about how their wives were always finding something else for them to do just when they thought they were finished for the day. They shared their preferences for cats over dogs, at least until they were proper old age pensioners and had more time, and then perhaps they might consider getting one. It was indeed a pleasant way to spend a morning and over far too soon as far as Frederick was concerned. It seemed as though they'd only just begun to know each other when they were gathering up their tools, testing the perfect swing of the re-hinged gate and getting ready to go to lunch.

"I say, Robert, can you tell me if there's a place nearby where a homesick Englishman can get a decent pint?"

"Aye, that'll be The Hare and Dog. The building goes back to the fifteenth century and has beautiful hand hewn timbers. That's where the townsfolk all go, and they do a proper roast dinner on a Sunday, too. Start baking the Yorkshires first thing in the morning, and every single one of them is gone by three. I've seen people line up out the door and down the street just to get a table."

"Well, then, will you allow me to buy you a pint some afternoon before we leave? Just us. Once in a while there are things you don't do with the wife. A pint with a mate in a dusty old pub, maybe a game of darts and eating the odd pickled egg, that's what I miss, Robert. Will you join me?"

Robert reached down and rubbed Thomas under the chin. "Aye, Frederick Watkins, I know what ye mean, and the answer is yes. You can get the first one, but only if you let me see to the second."

"What about today? I haven't much time, really. What have you got on for the afternoon?"

Robert explained he was planning to spend a bit of time sorting out the old van in the garage, but after that he wouldn't mind having the pint that Frederick had just offered. Frederick's scraggly eyebrows went skyward. He was immediately interested.

"Old van? Just exactly what kind of old van?

"An ancient Volkswagen, one of the first to come to England. It's got a pedigree almost as long as The Moorlands."

"Well, if you want to get a minute's peace, for heaven's sake don't let my wife know about it."

"What's that supposed to mean?"

"She's got an old VW van herself, not as old as this one, probably, but it's got some history. Loves it like one of her own, she does. Any chance she could take it out sometime? I know she'd love it. She's a very good driver."

Robert looked doubtful and shook his head. He was not a quick thinker, and he certainly hadn't planned on dealing with something like this. He spoke carefully.

"I wouldn't recommend it. She's probably not used to driving on our side of the road, and that thing can have a mind of its own some days. The roads here can be tricky, especially now when we can get a morning frost up in the hills. Let me think about it. Maybe one day on a flat road, and then only if someone goes with her."

"She'd love it," repeated Frederick.

Robert rumbled, rubbed his chin and then spoke. "I'll see what I can do, but first things first. How about tea time at the Hare and Dog for that pint?"

"Great. I'll meet you there. I think I'll go out for a walk beforehand. I haven't really had a chance to look around the village, and it will be getting dark before you know it."

"Don't get lost."

Frederick looked sheepish. "Oh, so you heard."

"Aye," said Robert, "Word gets around in a village."

"How well I wish I didn't know," laughed Frederick. "And now to completely change the subject, I wonder what's for lunch. The food here is great, simple English fare and plenty of it."

"Grand puddings, as well," said Mosely.

Frederick clapped a theatrical hand to his chest. "Blimey, I hope not! I had seconds last night."

A low chuckle sounded from somewhere deep in the center of Mosely's chest. "Been eating here for thirty years, and I've lived to tell the tale. Come on, then, we need to have a wash, or we'll get wrong."

"Aye," said Frederick.

While the others were at lunch, a grim-faced Margery Mosely was sitting alone at her desk. Her carefully constructed mission of almost thirty years duration was nearing its conclusion, and it was also in danger of coming apart at the seams. The very last thing in the world she needed was someone looking too closely at the books and asking uncomfortable questions. Embezzlement was one thing, but there was more to this story than money. Much more.

On the day she'd learned the humiliating truth about her mother's shameful birth and the cruel disdain with which Lord Gregory Ashton-Beckett had responded to desperate pleas for help when her grandmother was dying, Margery Mosely, then Margery Benton, had begun to plot her revenge. She was a methodical woman who considered the consequences of every word she said and everything she did. Thus far it had served her well, with no one in her immediate Moorlands circle being any the wiser. To them she was the bookkeeper, good with figures, well organized and a bit on the serious side. But that came with the territory, didn't it? You did your job, didn't you?

As far as the cook and the others knew, the undone or badly done tasks and the ill-timed breaking down of things were merely harmless pranks with a purpose. They were intended to convince a meddling new manager to stop fighting the tide of established tradition, resign from the position and thereby preserve their jobs.

She smiled at the memory of their cautious, then enthusiastic, compliance when she first explained it. They believed it was all about preserving beloved Moorlands traditions and, of course, their wages. They knew nothing about the hidden money or anything else that was, or had ever been, part of her long-term objective. No one, least of all her mild natured jack-of-all-trades husband Robert, knew the full extent of her duplicity, and she planned to keep it that way.

Good man that he was, she hadn't wanted to involve him at all. For thirty years he'd remained in blissful contented ignorance, tending to the buildings and the machines and the garden the whole time she was exacting her revenge.

It was because of Celia Attison's interference and investigations around the accounting that she'd been forced to tell him about the money and the need to terminate Celia's employment there as soon as possible. She alone knew the ends to which she'd already gone in her singular pursuit of the man who'd disgraced her grandmother and later turned away his own flesh and blood when illness struck and his own daughter came begging for help.

She was glad when she'd finally learned the truth that lay under the whispers she'd heard all of her life. Now she understood the dark looks and uncomfortable silences when the name Ashton-Beckett was mentioned. Now she knew why her grandmother had died in agony because the family couldn't afford a doctor. Now she understood the helpless fury her own mother experienced, sitting beside the bed and watching Margery's grandmother die.

Her own mother had literally worked herself to death to make a better life for Margery. She wanted to make a better life than the one she'd had as the daughter of a shamed woman, married in haste to a dull-witted man who wanted nothing more than someone to warm his bed and empty his chamber pot, a man who thought more of his animals than he did of Margery's mother.

When she first learned the truth of it all, Margery didn't know exactly how she would proceed, but she was determined and single minded. As she grew into womanhood, she never did know when that determination and single-mindedness became an obsession. As far as she could remember this was always part of who and what she was and what colored everything she did, but with each passing year the need for revenge grew stronger, and the time to exact it grew shorter.

That she and Robert had never had children was not an act of God. It was achieved through vigilance and careful planning. A child would get in her way. Robert never knew. He did question it from time to time, but when he did she would smile sadly, shake her head and say, "I suppose it just isn't meant to be, and I don't take with questioning nature. Our Thomas will do for now, won't you, Puss?"

Eventually he stopped asking.

Years before, when The Moorlands was first given over as a gift to the diocese, Lord Ashton-Beckett left the manor and moved with his family to a smaller house immediately adjacent to the property. Eventually, when his wife died and the children left home, Margery slipped quietly into his life. Shortly after she began work there, she invited her widower grandfather (unbeknownst to him) to take some of his meals in the big house so, she said, he wouldn't be lonely. When the old man could no longer get out and about, it was Margery who took him hot bread and fresh biscuits to enjoy with his tea, and it was Margery who made certain he never learned who she was.

Everyone in the village commented on how kindly she was and how nice that he could stay connected to the place where he grew up, but kindness had nothing to do with it. It was a simple and rather morbid curiosity. Margery wanted to know her grandfather, and she wanted him to know her. Later they said, wasn't it a shame that Margery had to be the one to find him sitting in his chair, cold and alone and very thoroughly dead?

A tap at the door wrenched Margery back to the present.

"Might I have a word, Mrs. Mosely?"

She looked up to see Annette Darcie standing in the doorway, looking anxious and twisting her apron.

Margery tried to keep the irritation off her face and out of her voice. "Yes of course, Annette. What seems to be the problem?"

"It's the new girl we hired last week. She and cook just had a horrible row in the kitchen, and she's walked out."

Margery pursed her lips and frowned. "I'm not the managing director, Annette, and she's not in today. You'll just have to go back and make do out there until she comes back. I do believe you've washed a dish or two in the past, have you not?"

Annette nodded.

"Well, then, I suppose you'll just have to add that to your list. We've all had extra work to do these days; no reason why you should miss out on your share, is there?"

"No, Mrs. Mosely."

"Thank you for letting me know, Annette. I'll be sure to tell Mrs. Attison."

Eleven

After lunch Richard Attison suggested the individual group members go off on their own and write down any and all thoughts, ideas and questions they might have about issues and challenges facing church leadership today. They could also go out for a walk and a bit of fresh air or, if they were so inclined, do both. The plan was to reconvene later in the afternoon for tea or sherry and discuss their ideas.

Olympia's first thought was to head straight for the sherry, but wisdom and overwhelming fatigue prevailed, and upon returning to their room, she crashed into her bed. Frederick tucked the duvet around her shoulders, picked up his latest book and crossword and took himself down to the sitting room. There he planned to spend a quiet hour or two reading or sleeping, or possibly a little of both, before walking down to the pub well in advance of Robert Mosely.

By midafternoon Celia was sitting up in bed and cautiously taking nourishment. More importantly, she was keeping it down. After the terrors, tremors and spasms of the previous night had finally ceased, she'd slept like the dead for almost five hours straight and was feeling much improved. When the first cup of tea and slice of dry toast stayed down, she spread orange marmalade on a second piece of toast, set it on the plate on the bed beside her and reached for her laptop. She knew it was best not to let the growing list of e-mails go unanswered, especially now with work being so difficult. She winced. The very thought of work produced a stomach spasm. She waited, and when nothing more happened she pushed the on-button, pulled up her mail and scrolled down to the message from the accountant. But before she could open it, the telephone rang; it was her husband inquiring after her health.

"I'm much better, Richard. I'll be really careful of what I eat, go to bed early tonight, and I should be back at my desk tomorrow. In fact, why don't I come in early so we can have breakfast together, and you can tell me how the conference is going? "

Richard agreed to the breakfast plan and related the events of the past twenty hours, including the facts that Olympia Brown had a nasty cold and Frederick had spent the morning with Robert Mosely, fixing the gate to the pasture. Then he asked what her plans were for the rest of the day.

"Not much. I'm just getting on to my e-mail," said Celia.

"Don't tire yourself now. Can't it wait until tomorrow when you get in?"

"I suppose it could, but I'll sleep better tonight if I can get some it out of the way today."

Richard agreed and thus assured, he wished her well and rang off.

Celia resettled herself against the pillows she'd piled against the headboard and opened the message. It was from Daniel Kaiser, ACA, an accountant she'd consulted the previous week without the board's knowledge or permission. She was not surprised to read that upon his initial examination of the financial records of the last five years, he'd discovered a number of perplexing irregularities and discrepancies. He offered nothing more but asked if there might be a time they could meet and discuss his findings.

Celia wrote back with thanks, saying she would check her calendar when she returned to work tomorrow and get back to him. Then she leaned back and stretched. There was no doubt she was feeling better internally, but the e-mail from the accountant left her with another kind of distress. It was becoming increasingly clear that her suspicions about financial irregularities were well founded, and she alone would be the one who could or would do anything about it. That was probably the most difficult part of this whole mess, feeling so alone while she tried to hold back the tide of something, but what was it? That's what she needed to find out. She wasn't sure if anyone on the board of directors would support her if she called for a full financial audit. She really needed someone on the inside she could trust, but did such a person exist? On the other hand, if she told no one and simply went ahead with this on her own and then presented the hard evidence, if there was any, to the governing board, then what? Go slowly, she told herself.

By now she was quite clear about who on the staff was on her side—probably no one other than Annette Darcie and maybe Bud Loring. There was no mistaking Margery Mosely's feeling for her. It was a clear case of the old queen, new queen syndrome. Margery had been in charge of all record-keeping for thirty years, and newcomer Celia had been there for just under six months. The keeper of the purse strings in any organization was in a powerful position, and people in power with longevity of tenure to support them were formidable opponents. But just how powerful was this woman? Certainly Celia could not have been the first person to want to review the record-keeping. She could feel her stomach twisting and forced herself to stop obsessing over something that was still in the early stages of inquiry. She would know a lot more when she met with Daniel Kaiser. Until then her best, and really her only, plan of action was to try and relax and get fully over whatever was ailing her.

With that decided, she was faced with another major decision, whether to shift her mind into neutral and play a game or five of solitaire or grit her teeth and open a few more e-mails. In the end she made a deal with herself: three rounds of solitaire, ten e-mails, and then get out of bed and find something a bit more substantial to eat.

In her own bed at The Moorlands, Olympia Brown was also feeling better. She rolled over, squinted at her watch and gave some thought to finding herself a cup of tea. It was a little after three in the afternoon, not quite tea or sherry time. She could wait.

"When in doubt, have a bath." It was one of her mother's many aphorisms which she heeded when it was convenient and ignored when it wasn't. She'd quickly learned that the English as a nation love their baths and therefore their bathtubs, particularly old ones with feet. The Moorlands had a spectacular bathtub. It was a great cast iron thing from another century that came all the way up to her armpits when she sat in it. Just the thing!

She looked around the room for something to read while in the tub and caught the light on her laptop winking at her from the desk in the corner. Olympia was almost powerless to resist its silent siren call but decided that a long hot bath, freshly washed hair and a change into clean clothes would make even the best of messages better ... maybe.

Almost an hour later, back in her room and wearing clean clothes, Olympia was much improved. Her toes and fingertips were still pink and wrinkled from their extended submersion, but it was clear she'd definitely turned some kind of a corner, thank heaven. All of this was compounded when she found messages from both Jim Sawicki and her daughter, Laura Wiltstrom, in her inbox. "Oh joy, oh rapture!"

Father Jim, best friend and colleague of long standing, was writing to say he had been officially received into the Episcopal Church. He went on to ask how she and Frederick were doing in the motherland, and was there a time they could have a Skype call and catch up in person, so to speak.

Laura's note was much the same as her last one. She was still settling in to a new locale, slowly making friends at work and finally feeling less lonely. Little Erica was increasing her vocabulary daily, and if Olympia knew how to do it, could they Skype sometime soon so she could see and hear for herself?

Olympia had to laugh. Two messages both with the same ending. Was this a cyberspace version of the handwriting on the wall? Well, she'd never Skyped before, but she was determined it was high time she mastered the skill—just not right now. Her brain was still mildly befogged by the retreating head cold. New computer learning required a good night's sleep, a fresh cup of coffee and a handy teenager. Surely there would be someone in the vicinity. Olympia stood, smoothed out her bed and started for the door.

Maybe I should go and ask Mrs. Mosely, she thought. She's been here since time began, and it's clear she's the go-to person around here. She might not be the nicest apple in the basket, but even cranky old apples benefitted from a little polishing. By way of response to her internal question, the clock on the bedside table chirped out a double chime, taking Olympia completely by surprise.

"What's that supposed to mean? Yes, go ask Mrs. Mosely, or yes, the sour-faced woman could do with a little flattery … or both?"

The clock had no further comment.

"Am I take that to mean I should pay attention, and this will be continued?"

Once again, the clock said nothing.

November 24, 1862
There is a cold rain falling, and by the look and feel it will likely turn to snow. Today at about mid-day there was a knock at the door, and a gentleman delivered a parcel addressed to me. When I opened the box I knew at once from whence it came. The box contained a clock, a small wooden clock I remember seeing on a shelf in Jared's office. When I commented upon it, he told me how much he valued that clock and the care he took when

winding it. He told me he especially liked the clear tone of the chime when it sounded. It had been a gift from his father when he took up his call to ministry. He said it was to be a constant reminder to cherish each and every minute God has seen fit to give him.

I confess that in the floods of tears I did not see the letter until later in the day when I had somewhat collected myself. Half hidden in the wrappings I discovered a short letter saying that this had been willed to me by the late Rev. Jared Mather, and it was to be given to Jonathan Mather Winslow. It was signed by an attorney whose name I have come to know.

I find it so very hard to look at, but little Jonathan is so enchanted by the sound of the chimes that I cannot hide it away. I did place it on a high shelf well out of his reach. There is so much that I will tell my little fellow when the time is right, but I do believe I see Richard coming to the kitchen door. I shall ask him to stay to dinner. It is dark outside, and no one will have seen him approach.

More anon. LFW

November 25, 1862

It is after midnight, and all is quiet. Richard did agree to stay for dinner. When Jonathan was safely in bed and Aunt Louisa was nodding over her knitting, we sat by the fire and talked. I should be abed myself, but sleep simply will not bless me so I turn again to pen and paper, my steady secret silent friend. I showed Richard the clock and told him how it came into my possession. He knows about Jonathan's father, and when I first learned of his passing from this life, Richard was a great comfort to me. He is such a good man and asks no more of me than to be his friend. This I can freely give and one day perhaps more, who can say. More than one unmarried lady in town has tried to catch his eye, and more than one well-intentioned neighbor has offered to introduce me to a bachelor friend. It can be both tiresome and awkward, but neither of us wishes to offend, and thus we smile and decline as gracefully as we are able.

    More anon, LFW

Twelve

After checking in with Olympia and finding her in good nick, Frederick, this time wearing a heavy jacket and armed with a proper English brolly, set off in the direction of the Hare and Dog. He was told he'd find it at the far end of the village of Little Humblesby, about a twenty minute walk due west from the manor house.

It would have been exactly that had Frederick walked at any kind of a pace. Instead he ambled, turning this way and that, taking in the country air and recharging his body and soul with the smells, tastes and sounds of his homeland. It was one of those one-road villages so common in rural England, bracketed by an old stone church and graveyard at one end and the local pub at the other.

On one side of the narrow street was a gently ascending terrace of small, well kept houses, and on the other was a procession of semi-detached houses set a little farther back from the road. Frederick could only assume, since there were no parked cars in sight, that villagers were all at work, or they kept their vehicles behind their houses.

Whatever the case, it made for easy and pleasant walking. In the familiar country way, people nodded and smiled, and the ever-present dogs nuzzled his hand when he passed by. It's good to be home, he thought, and wondered if Olympia might ever want to relocate to the UK. Then he asked himself a bigger question, and that was did he want to come back, or was all of this simply nostalgia for times gone by? This was still unanswered when he reached the pub, but he knew it would be waiting in the wings, and one day he would need to revisit it. No, they would have to revisit it.

Frederick pushed open the heavy hobnailed door to even more familiar sights and smells. The combined scents of beer and traces of cigarette smoke, which still lurked in the nooks and crannies of the crooked walls of the room even years after the ban, bore witness to the social history of the place. He stopped and stood just inside the door, taking it all in: the dusky quiet, the slanting late afternoon light, stools and small squat tables here and there and the polished bar at the far end of the room. Behind the bar there was one chalk board listing the daily specials and another announcing weekly quiz and trivia nights.

He was surprised to find it almost empty when the man behind the bar called out, "You just wait another half-hour, and they'll all be in. Regular as clockwork, they are, so you'd better speak up now. What can I get for you?"

"I've been living in the States for these last few years, so anything that is home grown and local will be wonderful. What would you recommend?"

"So y're a Geordie, are ye?"

"Is it that obvious?"

"Does a dog have bollocks? Come on then, and I'll pull y'a pint of our own Yorkshire bitter unless you have a mind for something else?"

Frederick laughed aloud at the graphic image, nodding an enthusiastic yes and holding out his hand for the brimming glass. "I'm Frederick Watkins, originally from the Northeast of England, more recently from the Northeast of the United States, and even more recently from The Moorlands up on the hill."

"What brings you back, then?" asked the friendly barman.

"My wife. She's an American, and she's over here doing a workshop as part of a clergy conference there. I found myself with some free time on my hands, so I thought I'd go for a walk and see a bit of the countryside."

"Y'didn't get very far then, did you?"

"Let's just say I followed my nose," rejoined Frederick.

This brought a hearty laugh from the other side of the bar, and an invitation to sit down and make himself comfortable.

"Have you lived here long?"

"This pub's been in my family for three generations. Does that answer your question? I was born and raised in these hills and dales and never saw fit to leave." He patted his broad chest in pride.

"Thank goodness some things haven't changed. To be honest, even though I've only been away a few years, now that I'm finally back it feels like everything is moving so much faster."

The barman shook his head. "It's not you. Even here in the land that man forgot and God remembered you can see it. Things are starting to change. People are moving closer to the cities. They don't want the village life anymore—too slow, too inconvenient, too far from work, not enough shops—and now there's the internet everywhere you look. Would you believe I had to put wi-fi in this place, or I would have been in trouble? The pub in the next village got it first, and all the young ones started going over there, the buggers. I had to get with the times, but I can't say I like it. People don't talk to each other anymore, they just sit and click."

Frederick nodded sympathetically. He was English. Tradition and keeping to the old ways was in his DNA. How often had he felt hopelessly out of touch with the world around him? Wisely he chose not to answer that question and parked it out of reach with the other one about moving back to England. With a start, he remembered he had a job to do. He rested both elbows on the bar and leaned forward, all wide-eyed and innocent, like an English fox.

"Tell me, if you've been here all your life and your father before you, you must remember when The Moorlands was a residence and not some kind of a religious hostel. I can only imagine what it must have been like then. Mind you, it's lovely and comfortable, and you can see how grand it was with its Adam fireplaces, molded ceilings and the like. But between you and me, it's getting a bit long in the tooth. Even I can see it, and my wife would tell you I'm not the most observant of men."

"Aye, the wives. They like us to think they see everything, and we let them. It's easier that way. Less arguing." He laughed and took up another glass to dry and polish.

Frederick was warming to his task. "So tell me about The Moorlands when it was grand. Did you know the family who lived there?"

"I knew of the Ashton-Beckett family, but none of us from this part of the county knew them in person. Too posh for us, they were, and they made damn sure we remembered it. Oh, yes, once a year they came round with baskets for the children at Christmas, and they made a big show of putting a socking great stained glass window in the church, but they didn't fool a one of us." He snorted and banged down the glass for emphasis, and then his expression changed from disgust to curiosity.

"Tell me, have you met a woman by the name Margery Mosely up there? I reckon she'd be about my age, in her mid-fifties. Like as not she works in the office."

Frederick deliberately kept his face neutral. "As a matter of fact, I have. Why do you ask?"

"Just wondered."

"Is she a friend of yours?" asked Frederick.

"It's a long story, far too long for now. It's going to get busy in here any minute. Maybe another time. It's not important, really, just old village gossip. I wondered if she was still there, that's all. "

"I've met her, but I couldn't tell you anything about her other than she seems a bit cheerless."

The barman nodded and reached for yet another glass. "Aye, that'll be her, all right. I wondered if she'd stay on there once the old man died."

Any hope of further conversation was ended with the snap of a latch and the creak of hinges followed by the sound of male voices. The two men looked up to see the first cluster of thirsty customers stumping through the door, and right behind them was Robert Mosely, looking most respectable. Gone were the faded overalls and wellies of the morning, and instead he was wearing sturdy, dark gray tweed trousers and an oversized green woolly. The man had obviously dressed for the occasion.

A rapidly improving Olympia found Mrs. Mosely seated at her desk, frowning at her computer. She stood waiting in the doorway, hoping the woman would look up and she wouldn't have to interrupt her. It didn't happen.

Olympia cleared her throat. "Excuse me, Mrs. Mosely, I wonder I could ask for some help."

The woman raised her eyes and peered at Olympia over the top of the monitor. "I don't have much time at the moment, Reverend Brown, but if you can tell me the nature of the problem, I'll see what I can do later on."

Olympia exhaled and relaxed. "I wondered if you know anything about using Skype? It's a kind of video picture telephone call thing you can do on your computer. I think it's one of those operations you understand if you're under twenty-five. I've managed to learn how to use e-mail and write my sermons, but anything beyond that is completely out of my comfort zone."

Margery Mosely did not look encouraging. "I'm afraid I've never had time for such modern foolishness, Reverend. It's all I can do to keep up with things the way they are now. I don't need any more of your so-called improvements and innovations, thank you very much."

Olympia clasped her two hands to her bosom and went into her most sympathetic and pastoral caring mode.

"I don't know how you manage it all, keeping tabs on a huge old place like this. So many things to keep track of: the guests, the housekeeping and hospitality, and all the time the cost of everything going nowhere but up. And that's not even taking into account the building and the grounds. It must be a nightmare."

"Not half. It's a day's work, I'll tell you."

"Well, it's clear you're the backbone of this place, Mrs. Mosely. If I had a hat, I'd tip it to you, but I don't so I'll get on with my search and not take up any more of your time. Thank you anyway."

Mrs. Mosely responded with what might have passed for a smile. "I'll think about it later on when I get a few minutes. There is someone in the village who tends to the office machines here. I'll ring him up. If he can't explain it to you, I'm sure he'll know someone who can."

Olympia returned the smile with interest. "That's really kind of you, Mrs. Mosely, but don't go to any trouble. It's not the end of the world if I don't learn how to do it. E-mail works just fine, and like you, I have more than enough to keep me busy right now."

"I wish more people around here understood that, Reverend Brown."

Olympia expanded her smile. "Oh, do please call me Olympia. Reverend sounds so formal and stand-offish."

"I'll do that, Olympia, and you may call me Margery."

"Thank you, Margery. I'll go and let you get back to your computing."

Olympia turned out of the office and started toward the sitting room. She was thinking of a song she used to sing with her boys about a farmer who had a dog. *B-I-N-G-O... B-I-N-G-O ... B-I-N-G-O and Bingo was his name-o!* Check off step one, Olympia, you've gotten your toe past the chain-link fence surrounding Margery Mosely.

Thirteen

When Olympia stepped into the sitting room she found Steve Warner and Rosemary Lewis seated next to each other near the fire. They were deep in conversation and didn't hear her open the door. As she stepped over the threshold she deliberately scraped her shoe and rattled the papers in her hands to alert them to her presence and watched as they moved apart and looked in her direction.

"Do you mind if I join you, or is this private?"

Rosemary beckoned her closer. "Oh, gracious no, Olympia. I'm so glad to see you're feeling better. Do come and join us, it's so cozy by the fire. Would you like a cup of tea? I was just talking about getting us one, wasn't I, Steve?"

Olympia shook her head. "No, thank you. I think I'm tea-ed out. One more mouthful and I'll start growing fins and gills."

Rosemary smiled. Steve chuckled and said he really needed to get cracking on the day's assignment before they reconvened later on.

"Don't leave on my account," implored Olympia.

He held up his hand and shook his head. "Not at all. I'm a bit of a procrastinator, and talking shop with a favorite colleague is such a luxury that when I get the chance, I'm afraid I'm likely to overindulge. I really must be going. See you later, both of you."

When Steve closed the door Rosemary turned to Olympia and began to ask questions about her ministry in the United States. For the next hour they sat with their feet stretched toward the fire and compared issues with aging congregations, types of ministry, hospital chaplaincy and hospice work. Then they went on to compare similarities and differences in preparation for professional ministry in the two countries and the need and nature of pastoral care. Olympia found it all very interesting, and she was finding Rosemary Lewis very interesting, as well. The two had much in common. Rosie, as she asked to be called, was an intelligent woman with a warm and open personality. A divorced mother of an almost grown daughter, like Olympia, she'd been on her own for years. She was a woman who had to make the most of her time and knew how to do it.

Olympia felt an instant kinship with the woman but wisely said nothing for the moment. She needed to remember that even though they were both mid-life women who had raised children mostly on their own, Olympia was a facilitator as well as a colleague, and this was England not the USA. She'd already learned that lines of socialization and communication were vastly different here, and for once in her ebullient and enthusiastic life she was not going to act the part of the outrageous American bull in an English china shop. It was enough for today to listen to each other's stories and commiserate over single parenthood and the challenges of pastoring a congregation. Then Rosemary reached over and put her hand on Olympia's arm. She spoke in a low voice.

"Not now, because everyone will be back here in just a few minutes, but I wonder if I might have a word alone with you sometime this week?"

Olympia covered Rosemary's hand with her own. "Of course. We could sit together at breakfast or lunch tomorrow or Wednesday. You tell me."

"No, "said Rosemary a little too sharply. "Not here. Maybe we could go for a walk or maybe over to the pub, somewhere we won't be interrupted."

"Sure, I ..."

They were prevented from any further discussion on the subject by the chatter and clatter of the rest of the conferees, including Steve Warner, coming into the room. They were calling out greetings to one another and dragging chairs and

cushions closer to the fire. Olympia was happy that Richard
Attison was in charge of this session. Her only job today was to
listen and ask clarifying questions. I can do this, she thought,
although yesterday it would have been completely beyond me.
She was feeling profoundly grateful for her improving state of
health. At the same time she was curious about what it was
Rosemary Lewis wanted to talk with her about that was so very
private. She looked over to where Rosemary was seated, pen in
hand, staring at the open notebook in her lap. The woman was
troubled, but would or could Olympia be able to help?

When all were assembled and seated, Richard asked if each
one of them would take turns sharing what they'd come up with
on the subject of issues and challenges surrounding church
leadership.

As they did so Olympia found it all too distressingly
familiar: too much power in too few hands, church bullies and
matriarchs insisting on control, dwindling attendance, and
crushing and skyrocketing maintenance and administrative costs.
She asked herself, as she often did back home, is there any room
for God in any of this—and when did religion become a business
and a numbers game rather than a healing and caring community
of the spirit? Over twenty years in ministry and she still didn't
have an answer, but one thing was becoming clear. Church
leadership needed to include, and therefore train, more lay
people.

She planned to address this very thing for most of tomorrow
in a session entitled, "Releasing Your Inner Sermon." It was a
workshop she'd offered a number of times in the States, but this
time the emphasis would be on showing those present how to
teach and develop the skill to lay people in their home
congregations. Her mind was drifting. She pulled herself back to
the present and noticed for the second time today the energy
arcing between Rosemary and Steve. She wondered if that was
what Rosemary wanted to talk about. Olympia knew Rosemary
was divorced, but what about Steve?

"Olympia, what are your thoughts about using a business model for church administration and doing away with the committee approach?" Richard Attison was speaking to her.

"Huh?"

He repeated the question.

"I plead the fifth."

"I don't understand."

"I'm sorry, Richard, my mind wandered. I'll be running on full power tomorrow, I promise."

The last half of her sentence was lost in the clanging of the dinner bell. As the conference members were collecting their things and getting ready to leave the room, Olympia remembered she needed some electronic assistance and called out, "Say, while you're all still here, is there anyone who could show me how to use Skype?"

Steve Warner held up his hand. "I have a fourteen-year-old son at home. He taught me. I can show you how to do it tonight after dinner, if you'd like."

"I accept, and I'll even bring the wine," said Olympia.

In a back corner of the Hare and Dog, Robert Mosely and Frederick Watkins were well into their second pint. With Frederick's subtle encouragement they'd talked about childhood wartime memories, first cars, early schooling, first jobs, and were just getting on to marriage and the nature of women in general when Robert looked up at the clock on the wall. "Uh oh, we're going to be late for dinner."

"Is that going to be a problem?" asked Frederick.

Mosely rubbed his chin before responding. "I suppose not. It's just that I didn't tell her. She'll be expecting me. Right bugger for detail, she is, wants to know where everything is at all times. No surprises for our Margery."

"I'll tell you what. I really fancy a steak and kidney pie and another pint. Will you join me? I don't mind not listening to conference talk while I eat. It's not like we're driving. Do you think she'll mind?"

It was clear that Robert Mosely was conflicted, but Frederick knew he might not have this kind of an opportunity again, so uncharacteristically, he pressed his case.

"I'm going to stay on either way. I didn't realize how much I missed the everyday life of England. America is wonderful, and I'll most likely end my days there, but a pint and a pie in a local pub is simply not an option there. I'd be most indebted to you if you could stay on."

"What about your missus?"

"I told her we were going out for a pint. She knows I can take care of myself."

It worked. Mosely pulled out his phone and stepped to the door of the pub, and Frederick let out a long slow breath of relief. When he returned Frederick ordered his steak and kidney pie, and Robert decided on bangers and mash. Frederick went up to the bar and ordered their food and came back with two more pints.

"Are ye tryin' to get me drunk, Frederick Watkins?" Mosely grinned and held out a willing hand.

"Not with all the food I just ordered. We'll be here a while longer, and I don't want to be thirsty, and I don't like to drink alone. Thank you for staying on. You've made me a happy man."

"It doesn't take much, then," said Robert with an easy grin.

"Not much at all, I'm a simple man. Now, where were we? I think we had just started on the fair sex, if I remember. I'm not sure if I told you, but Olympia and I have only been married for four months. We met a couple of years ago when I went to the States on holiday. I must say, however, it took me a while to convince her to say yes."

Robert took a long swallow out of his glass. "Margery and I have been married for thirty-three years. Thirty of those years we've lived and worked at The Moorlands. She keeps the accounts, and I fix things, but I think I told you that this morning by the gate." He belched discreetly behind his fist and begged Frederick's pardon.

Frederick leaned forward, putting both elbows on the table. "Thirty years in the same place. I'll bet you've seen a lot of changes."

"Not half," said Mosely.

"Did you ever think you'd want to work somewhere else?"

"Once or twice, but the wife wouldn't hear of it, so here we are. I'm not one to complain. It's a good life."

"But you say things are changing."

"Aye, that they are," said Robert Mosely, "that they are."

Frederick paused and selected his words with care. "I have a question for you. From your perspective of a long marriage to the same woman and the same job for almost as long, what words of wisdom do you have for a man who's just gotten married and is starting over?"

Mosely looked up toward the ceiling as he considered his answer.

"Don't assume anything. Things aren't always what they seem."

"Are you taking the mickey? What's that supposed to mean?"

Mosely chuckled and shook his head. "No. What I mean is, no matter how well you think you know someone, you probably don't know everything, and perhaps it's best if you don't."

Now it was Frederick's turn to chuckle and nod sympathetically. "I think most of us have a few things in our past that are probably best left unsaid, wouldn't you say?"

"Aye, and some more than others, but look sharp, here comes our food."

"And not a minute too soon," said Frederick. "I think I've been waiting three years for this meal."

The aproned waiter set their steaming plates on the table and asked if there was anything else they needed. Frederick shook his head; too busy inhaling the scents and admiring the symmetry of the achingly familiar feast before him. Frederick Watkins was a happy man.

After supper and her Skype lesson, Olympia turned in early and was deeply asleep when Frederick returned. He smiled over at her recumbent form, watching the rhythmic rise and fall of her shoulders. That's my woman, he thought, and then he wondered what, if any, secrets she might be harboring. I'll ask her when we get up tomorrow … or then again, maybe I won't.

Fourteen

When dawn's early light slipped through the gap in the window curtains, Olympia was happy to greet it. She was feeling better, so much better that she seriously considered waking Frederick, but she realized she had no idea how soundproof the walls were or how squeaky the beds. This probably needed a bit of research before she raised his, er, hopes. For now, although a poor substitute, hot coffee and a full English breakfast would have to suffice.

She pulled on her clothes and tossed an extra sweater over her arm just as Frederick crested the duvet. His wispy hair was a fright.

"Up and off so soon, my love?"

"I thought I'd go check my e-mail and, while I'm at it, set Skype dates with Laura and Jim. How did your evening with Robert Mosely go? Do you know any more than when you left?"

"Not really. There didn't seem to be a lot of lines I could read between. He's a pretty straightforward bloke. If there is something untoward going on here, I'll bet you a pound to a hayseed he has nothing to do with it."

Olympia giggled at the very English analogy. It was one she hadn't heard before. She was still learning new things about this man she married, and so far it was all to her liking. She smiled. "Coffee, Frederick, I need coffee. Breakfast is in an hour, but they put the coffee and tea out at seven. I should be through my correspondence by then, and you can fill me in over breakfast."

"Okay, but there's not much to tell. He's a bit of a plodder. A good man, takes his orders from his wife and loves to potter about. The job's perfect for him. He's unschooled, but he's got a keen intelligence when it comes to fixing things. He can sort out just about anything on the property. He likes the challenge, and he likes that there's so much to do here. Someone else would think that was a problem, but not him. It's his meat and gravy."

"Tell me the rest later, darling."

Frederick was going to say there wasn't that much more to tell, but she was already out the door.

"Bloody Americans," he grumped, "always in a rush."

Armed with a brimming cup of freshly brewed, hot black coffee (She couldn't tolerate instant under any circumstances.), Olympia shut the door of the internet room behind her and sat down at one of the desks. After a long sip of her coffee and a sigh of contentment, she powered up her computer. Thus fortified, she first deleted the flotsam and jetsam and then fired off e-mails to Laura, Jim and both her sons. She told them she was now Skype-conversant and asked for a mutually good time to show off her skills. After that she checked the *USA Today* news headlines and the weather for southeastern New England, and she still had a half-hour before breakfast would be served. After two days of not wanting to eat, her stomach was signaling her return to health, and she was really hungry.

I wonder if I can talk the cook out of a little something before the bell, she thought, and while I'm at it, maybe get the recipe for that sticky toffee pudding she made. Olympia started salivating at the mere thought of it. She pushed back her chair, shut down her computer and set off toward the dining room and a persuasive encounter with the cook.

When she entered the room she went straight to the serving window and found the cook standing at the Aga, glowering at the porridge bubbling in a pot the size of which Olympia had never seen before. It was huge.

"Good morning, Mrs. Loring. If you're not too busy, I wonder if I could ask you a question."

"I am busy, but I can hear you. What's your question?"

Olympia was not prepared for such a brusque response but stood her ground and carried on.

"Well, its two questions really. Do you think I might have a piece of toast or a bit of fruit before the breakfast bell? I've been sick for the last two days, and along with my health, my appetite has returned, and I'm famished."

She nodded. "The bread's out by the toaster, so go help yourself. That's one question. What's t'other one?"

Olympia gulped and put on her most winsome and appealing smile. "The night I got here you made something called sticky toffee pudding."

Mrs. Loring never took her eyes off the pot. "Aye."

"To be honest, I never in my life had anything so delicious. I thought I'd died and gone to heaven. I don't suppose you'd ever teach me how to make it?"

At that Mrs. Loring stopped stirring and looked at Olympia, and she actually smiled. "That good, was it?"

Olympia clasped her hands to her chest and shut her eyes in a mock swoon."

"Well, then, I suppose I'll just have to do it, won't I? Can't have you fainting on the floor, can we? Come see me after lunch, it won't take long. Bring a pencil, and you can copy out the recipe."

"That's two," Olympia said half aloud to herself.

"What was that?" called the cook, still stirring the pot.

"Uh, I said it's very kind of you. I'll just go make myself a piece of toast and not bother you anymore."

"If you've been poorly, then you need more than toast. There's eggs in the dish on the long table. They're fresh this morning, I just boiled them."

"Why, thank you, Mrs. Loring."

"No need to thank me, I'm just doing my job."

The cook went back to her porridge, and Olympia went off in search of the hardboiled eggs and some toast.

Well, I've made some sort of progress on that front, she thought. I'll know how much this afternoon if I can get anything more out her than the sticky toffee pudding recipe. Even if I can't, that in itself will be a triumph. I'm going to put it on this year's Christmas dinner menu and then sit back and bask in its reflected glory. Wisely she left the astronomical calorie count out of her line of vision.

Olympia was deep in thought, as well as into her eggs and toast, when the dining room opened for breakfast. First in was Rosie Lewis, who came straight over and asked if she could join her.

"Of course. Here, let me move my stuff over to the other side."

"I'll go and get myself a cup of tea and something to eat."

She was soon back and settled when they were joined by Steve Warner. "Is this seat taken?" He indicated the seat on the other side of Rosie.

"I do believe I see your name on it," said Olympia.

He set his satchel down on the floor beside the chair and, like Rosie, went off in search of sustenance. Before long most of the members of the conference were seated around their two allotted tables, and the room was buzzing with the clinking of eating utensils and the soft hum of pleasant conversation.

Confident she couldn't be heard over the voices, Olympia leaned over and whispered in Rosie's ear, "Shall we take ourselves off to the pub for lunch today?"

Rosie shook her head and whispered back. "No, someone could ask to join us, and we can't very well say no, can we? Why don't we save some bread and cheese from breakfast and take ourselves off for a walk at lunchtime? I'm sure we can find a pleasant spot."

"Good idea," said Olympia turning back to her breakfast. Now she was really curious. Rosie wasn't wasting any time arranging a time for them to talk, nor was Steve Warner wasting any time in finding a way to sit near Rosie. No, she wasn't imagining it; something was going on here. This could be a good thing, or it could be disastrous. It all depends on the circumstances—and if you think about it, doesn't everything?

Fifteen

Celia woke up feeling one hundred percent better and more than ready to take on the day and whatever awaited her at The Moorlands. She was so glad Richard had called on Olympia Brown to come on board. She liked the woman, and her very presence there, hers and Richard's, made Celia feel like she wasn't alone. Now there were at least two people on her side, and three if she could count Annette Darcie.

She was almost out the door when she had a change of mind and returned to her desk. She pulled a card out of her handbag and dialed the number of Daniel Kaiser, ACA. If there was something seriously amiss in the accounting system, wouldn't it be far better to confront it right away when she had two allies on site and in her corner?

It was a rhetorical question.

Daniel Kaiser picked up on the second ring. After identifying herself she told him that upon further consideration of his e-mail, she'd decided to act on this as soon as possible, and did he have any available time today?

Whether it was the urgency in her voice or the seriousness of the situation, he said he could arrange to see her at ten that very morning. He went on to say it shouldn't take too long, but given the impending consequences of inaction, the sooner they could get on to it the better. Celia was both gratified to learn they were on to something and deeply troubled at the implications of what she'd just heard. She accepted at once, thanked him and rang off.

Now what? Should she call in and say she'd be late? No. Simply arrive late and carry on as though nothing were wrong? No. Call Richard? Yes. She looked at her watch. It was 9:00

a.m., and the accountant's office was at least an hour's drive away. She'd have to give it a bit of welly if she was going to be there on time. She smiled. A hard fast drive would actually relax her. She just needed to be sure not to get ticketed again.

At 10:05 a.m. Celia was seated across the desk from Daniel Kaiser, and neither of them was looking pleased. After the ritual greeting formalities, Kaiser was the first to speak.

"Thanks to modern technology, Mrs. Attison, my IT person was able to examine the accounts of The Moorlands thoroughly, and she seems to have discovered a major irregularity."

"What might that be?" Celia was wiggling her foot under her chair. It was a nervous habit of years.

"Well, you do understand that the electronic records you provided me with only go back five years, so that's all we have to work with; but even with that little it would appear significant monies are being paid to a service provider which doesn't exist. It this case it's UK Hospitality Services LTD. What do you know about them?"

Celia was initially speechless, but within seconds she recovered and reclaimed her voice.

"I ... I suppose I don't really know anything. Mrs. Mosely gives us all an accounting sheet every month. We never question her, because she's been doing it for so long. I think I once asked who they were and what we got from them, and she said lots of people used them these days. They were a major supplier for the medical and hospitality industries. They provided everything from linens and uniforms, to wholesale foods, to casual maintenance and service staff. One-stop shopping is the way she put it, very efficient and by far the best prices. I thought she'd done us a favor by finding them."

"Sadly, Mrs. Attison, it's one of the oldest tricks in the book—ahem, no pun intended. All it takes is a very clever, meticulous and persistent person. Usually it starts with a very small amount here and there, and if that isn't detected, then the embezzler gets bolder and takes more and more. A false vendor is often used to siphon significant funds out of an operating budget without detection. People like this get caught when they get too greedy or when a sharp-eyed manager like yourself puts two and two together and comes up with a negative sum."

"I don't know what to say. What do I do now? Who do I tell?" Celia was shaking her head and wringing her hands.

"Quite frankly, I suggest you do absolutely nothing at the present."

"But …"

"Please hear me out. I've only seen five years' worth of accounts, perfectly kept, I might add. I can be almost certain there is more to be uncovered but only if we can have access to the financial records going all the way back to when The Moorlands first incorporated as a charitable institution. Will that be possible, and if so, how soon can you get them to me?"

Celia shook head in disbelief and in sad acknowledgment that she'd undoubtedly cracked the problem of why The Moorlands was almost bankrupt. By now she was virtually certain who was responsible, but why? Why would a woman with a good natured husband, a nice place to live and a job she could have until she chose to retire, kill the golden goose, so to speak?

"How soon will you need those books, Mr. Kaiser? I'm not exactly sure where they are. The Moorlands went electronic about five years ago, but I'm relatively new to the job. The only person who would know where they are is the bookkeeper, Mrs. Mosely, and I'm not at all sure she's going to want to hand them over to me."

Kaiser looked at Celia over his glasses and began tapping his fingers on the top of his desk. "Does she have any choice? You are the managing director, are you not? Simply tell her to bring you the books."

"Technically you are correct, Mr. Kaiser, but you don't know this woman. She's never been easy to work with. She's as precise as they come, never a paper or a pencil out of order on her desk, and she's had total control over the accounts for thirty years. Nobody's ever questioned her because, well, until now there was nothing to question."

"Nothing any of you thought to question, Mrs. Attison. But you can't blame yourself. This has been going on for a lot longer than five years, that much I can tell you."

Celia, now slumped in her chair, nodded miserably.

"Keep this in mind: whoever has done this stands innocent until proven guilty. Even if you are virtually certain you know who it is, you can't make an accusation. You can't say anything until we have the whole picture."

"And then what?"

"First you take the facts and figures in full to the board of directors, and you let them take it from there. Then it's their job, not yours. Once that is accomplished, we need to find out where all that money is hidden. It's got to be somewhere."

"All that money? So you think it's a fair amount then?"

"If this has been going on for almost thirty years, it could easily be in the hundreds of thousands of pounds, Mrs. Attison. Now do you see why we need those books?"

Celia straightened up in her chair, flushed with anger and outrage. "I'll get them for you, Mr. Kaiser."

When she was back in her car and steaming over the hills towards The Moorlands, she kept trying to make sense of it all. The whole meeting, one that would change her life and that of everyone connected to The Moorlands, had taken less than forty minutes. She glanced at the clock on the dashboard. If I step on it, she thought, I can get back before lunch.

Back in the conference room at the retreat center, the morning was going well. The members of the group were as eager to improve and expand their own sermon writing as they were to learn how best to develop and encourage others in their congregations. We ministers do like the sounds of our own voices, me included, thought Olympia. But it doesn't matter how well we can pronounce the words, the message has got to have some substance, or it isn't worth the paper it's written on.

By "elevenses" each person in the room had said what their most and least favorite sermon topics were and why that was so. The assignment for the rest of the morning after the break was to outline two sermons, one on a preferred subject and another on a disagreeable one. The people in the room were a very intelligent, and sometimes very naughty, group. Therefore, it was no surprise to Olympia when they put on a good display of theatrics, histrionics and even a few risqué suggestions about what might make good sermon topics.

Olympia was in top form, and she knew it. Across the room she could see Richard Attison beaming his approval. This is just what he said he wanted to happen this week, and by God, she was doing it. It was the secondary assignment she wasn't so sure about and wondered if and when she might have another chance to talk with Celia. Later today she'd chat up the cook and get one hell of a recipe, but anything else was an unknown quantity. So what was she really looking for? While the group members were outlining their topics, Olympia took herself out of the room to locate a cup of tea and do a little mind-clearing.

There was no doubt in her mind that there was tension and dissension between Celia and members of the housekeeping, maintenance and administrative staffs; but where were the lines, and who had drawn them? Who is on what side of the issue, and more importantly, what exactly *is* the issue? Is it that The Moorlands is in imminent danger of closing its doors for good? Or is the real question why is it in such a predicament? If that's the case, then who or what is behind it and for what reason?

Olympia slowly walked back to the conference room, sipping at her tea and going over what she knew so far. Celia had told her there seemed to be a discrepancy in the accounting. If that was found to be so, then it could only be Mrs. Mosely who could understand and explain it. On the other hand, there was clearly a morale problem here, as well. Would that bankrupt a place? Olympia supposed it could if it was so bad that people no longer wanted to come here and make use of the place. What about health and safety? The place is certainly in need of major repair. If word got around that the place was not up to modern building code regulations, it could be shut down in short order.

She looked at her watch and wondered if Celia would be in today and, if so, when? Olympia's thoughts were beginning to focus, and it was time to ask Celia Attison some very direct questions.

When she opened the door of the conference room, all was silence except for the sound of intense scribbling. Rather than disturb anyone, she tiptoed over to where Richard Attison was sitting and touched him on the shoulder. When she had his attention she whispered, "Has Celia come in yet?"

He shook his head and spoke behind his hand. "She called me right after breakfast. She's meeting with an accountant right now. She said she'd try and be back right after lunch. I didn't know she'd actually contacted one. That's one on me."

Olympia squeezed her eyes shut and gulped. "Then I need to talk to you before she gets here."

Richard gave a brief nod and went back to his own scribbling. Olympia carried her tea back to her chair and curled herself into it. It had been her understanding until this very minute that Celia was planning to consult an accountant, as in future tense. Now she was actually out there doing it, right now, present tense. Now what? Whether this was a good or a bad move, it was damn sure an unexpected one, and it could change the whole landscape.

Olympia had the uncomfortable feeling things were rapidly gyrating out of control. She had come here with the understanding that she would be an observer. Would that still be possible if Celia came back and blew the roof off everything? If some sort of financial sabotage had been discovered, that could happen as early as this afternoon. Damn! I need to get to her before she says anything, Olympia fretted, and I've gone and committed myself to going for a walk with Rosie. Olympia's mind was in overdrive and picking up speed.

The midday lunch bell signaled the end of the morning's work and gave Olympia the chance to pull Richard aside before he got out of the room.

"Can you call Celia and ask her not to say anything to anyone until we three can hear what she's learned?"

"I can try, but she usually won't pick up if she's driving. She drives like a bat out of hell, but most of the time she's wise enough not to talk on the phone while doing it."

"Well, then, maybe you could call and leave her a message."

"Tell you what. I'll leave her a voice mail on all three phones—cell, office and the one at home. I'll also leave a note on her desk, asking that she find me the minute she gets in."

"That should do it. You know her better that I do. If she is the bearer of bad tidings, is she likely to blurt it out as she comes through the door?"

"Not usually," said Richard.

The two were both startled and interrupted by Celia herself.

"Richard, Olympia, I need a word … now." Her voice was tight, and she was flushed.

"Give me a minute to make my apologies to Rosie Lewis. I assume we'll be meeting in your office?"

She shook her head. "Not a good idea. I'll be waiting in my car. It's parked out in front."

Sixteen

It took Olympia less than two minutes to join the others in Celia's bright blue Ford Fiesta. Richard had seated himself in the back so the two women could talk more easily. They were barely belted in when Celia stepped on the gas, turned right and slipped onto the main road.

"Were you able to tell Frederick you were going out for a little while?" asked Richard.

"I didn't see him, but I told Rosie Celia had something she wanted to show me, and this was the only time she could do it. I asked her if she would please tell Frederick if she happened to see him."

"She was all right with that?" said Celia.

"She seemed to be. I said I would make time for our walk this afternoon."

"What's that all about then?" asked Richard.

"I don't know. Rosie asked if she could have a private word with me. She didn't say about what."

"If it's private, then I won't ask, but I think I've got a pretty good idea."

Before Olympia could say anything more on the matter, Celia signaled and whipped off to the left and into a church car park. She pulled up to the gate to the cemetery, set the hand brake, and rolled down the windows to let in some fresh air. She didn't waste any time getting right down to her business.

"I haven't told anyone at The Moorlands about this. That's why I thought we should have this conversation in a place where we couldn't possibly be overheard."

"This is beginning to sound really serious," said her husband.

"Not half. I have the feeling it's much more than workplace politics or a personality conflict, and we've only just started looking into it. If what Daniel Kaiser suggested to me this morning is true, then whoever is responsible will likely be facing imprisonment."

"Good heavens! What did he say?" asked Olympia.

"Let me start at the beginning." Celia undid her seatbelt and turned so she could more or less address them both.

"I began to get seriously concerned about the accounting about two months ago. So much so that I suggested the board consider calling for a full audit as a way to find out why we were in such precarious financial shape. Margery Mosely was at the meeting; she always attends as an ex-officio member. Well, she all but exploded. Got all huffy and even teary eyed. Said no one had ever questioned her before, and didn't she bring in a report that matched perfectly with the records on file to every meeting of the board?"

"What happened then?" asked Olympia.

"I was afraid we were going to have to send out for smelling salts and brandy to calm her down. All of a sudden I was the villain, and she was the wounded heroine. We spent the rest of the meeting assuring her that no one was questioning her integrity or her value to the institution and promising never to question her again."

"And the matter was dropped?" asked Richard.

"Like a hot cake, but it got me thinking. So one day, when I knew she was away, I sat down at her computer and went into the accounts file."

"What did you find?"

"Nothing—well, nothing that looked out of order. It was perfect, but then Margery is perfection personified. I believe the term is obsessive compulsive. She really gets out of her pram if anything is out of order. Everything has to be in its place, and

God help the witless individual who leaves anything out where she can find it. You should see her desk. But I'm getting off the point. The more I looked at the figures, the more I sensed something was amiss. As I said, everything was perfect—too perfect, but I didn't really know what I was looking for."

"So how did you get all that to the accountant?" By now Olympia and Richard were hanging on every word.

"I waited until she was out for a couple of hours, and I downloaded it all onto a flash drive. Then I did it a second time on a different one, just in case I lost or misplaced the first one. I knew I was not likely to get another chance. Margery Mosely has no idea."

"Good thinking. So what did he find?"

When Celia finished telling them all she'd just learned, she looked empty and shrunken like a deflated balloon.

"So how do we get the earlier books?" asked the ever practical and get-right-to-the-point Olympia.

"That is the million dollar question. I have no idea where they might be, but I do know that Margery never throws anything out. Oh, she keeps it all neat, but I swear to God, that woman probably still has her baby shoes and every pair since. So it stands to reason she's probably got the books packed away somewhere."

"That's in our favor," said Olympia.

"That's about all that is." Celia was still badly shaken.

"You said Margery has no idea?"

"I don't think so, Olympia. The whole idea of an audit was tabled two months ago. Oh, but wait a minute. I did say I planned to bring it up again at the next board meeting, only it was cancelled without my say-so. I was furious. Now that I think about it, she well may have been the one who scuttled it."

"Did Margery see you when you came back today?"

"Only briefly."

"Did you say anything about this to her?"

"Absolutely not. She made a great show of asking if I was feeling better, as if she gave tuppence."

"What did you tell her?" said Olympia.

"I said I thought so."

"So what do we do now?" asked her husband.

"I suppose we go back and try and find those books."

"Is it possible she might have put all the older records on another file that's backed up somewhere on her computer? You said she was meticulous. Do you think she might have set up another file somewhere, maybe even on a different computer she's got somewhere else?"

Celia shook her head in defeat and despair. "I suppose anything's possible, but I have absolutely no idea where to begin looking or how. I'm not exactly a technical genius. I can do the basics but not much more."

Olympia held up her hand. "Hang on. I might just have an idea. It's going to sound pretty far-fetched, but right now we have little or nothing in our corner, so almost anything is worth a shot, right? I do know someone who, if he can't tell me how to start looking for it, certainly knows someone who does."

"Who might that be?" asked Richard. He was not looking convinced.

"Have I ever told you about my best friend in the world, Father Jim Sawicki?"

"Can you tell us on the way back? I think we need to get moving. I don't want to do anything to raise any eyebrows."

"Sure can," said Olympia. "It's a long story I can tell in five minutes or less. If you ever come to the States, you'll have to meet him."

Celia turned the key and started the car. "Let's get this little dilemma out of the way before we consider international travel. I've got my hands full just now, don't you think?"

When they got back to The Moorlands, Olympia caught Celia by the arm and pulled her aside before they went through the door.

"I've just had a very unpleasant thought."

"To be honest, I don't think I can take in much more. Can't it wait?"

"Tell me something. This stomach ailment of yours, does it only happen when you're at work?"

Celia looked thoughtful and then puzzled. "As a matter of fact, yes. I wondered about that myself, but the doctor said it was probably stress."

"I'm thinking I'm not so sure about that."

"Are you an MD as well as a PhD?"

"Hardly, but what I am suggesting is a little experiment."

"And that is?"

"Don't eat anything at The Moorlands that you haven't prepared and carried in yourself. Don't make a big thing about it, just do it. If your weekly bouts of illness are stress related, they won't go away, but if they are caused by something you are eating here, they will."

"That's a terrible thought."

"No kidding. From what I can see in the few days I've been here, someone, or a couple of someones, are doing everything to discredit you and make you look unfit for the job. Getting unpleasantly and embarrassingly sick a lot would certainly paint that kind of a picture, would it not?"

Celia nodded slowly as Olympia's words began to make sense. "I'm afraid it would," she said, "Thank you for the warning."

On her way to the dining room, Olympia walked straight into Margery Mosely.

"Oh, hello there, Margery, have you seen my husband?"

She nodded and then added the barest hint of a smile to accompany it. "I wouldn't be surprised if he's out in the garage with my husband Robert. He had some work to do on the van. The starter seems to be playing up, and he's not sure if it's a fuse or summat more serious like a cable. He knows his cars, does my Robert."

"Van? What kind of van?" Olympia was immediately interested.

"Piece of history, I'll tell you; it's an old Volkswagen, one of the first to come to England. It came with the property when the old man gave it over to the diocese."

"Did I hear you correctly, an old Volkswagen? I have an old VW at home. It's about twenty years old. I adore that thing. Do you suppose they'd mind if I went out and had a look?"

"Suit yourself. A car is a car as far as I'm concerned, as long as they go and they stop when they are supposed to. That's all I expect."

"Oh, I think cars have personalities. I know my van does." Olympia was all but jumping up and down in anticipation.

Margery waved her away. "Off with you then, but don't be surprised if you don't get a word out of them. They're in a whole different world out there."

"Oh, I won't bother them just now. I'm off to the computer room."

Seventeen

Olympia went off to collect her computer and then back down to the internet room. Come hell or high water, she was going to connect with her children and Jim. It had been far too long. She looked at her watch. It was 1:00 p.m. UK time, which meant it was 8:00 a.m. back home and 5:00 a.m. in California, if her reckoning was right.

She was pleased to find the internet room empty, both for the nature of the conversations she planned to have and to spare herself the embarrassment of stumbling her way through Skype with an audience. As luck would have it, or perhaps there was a special saint in charge of electronic communication, after a few bleeps, dings and burps she was actually looking at her daughter, bleary eyed but awake.

"Laura!"

"Wow! You did it! Hold on, I'll go get Erica, she's an early riser, too."

Olympia found herself distracted at seeing her own image on the screen but soldiered on. Then her daughter returned, holding a wiggly little clad in pink, bunny-feet pajamas.

"Say hi to Grandma, honey."

The baby said nothing but instead stretched her chubby little hand toward the screen, and it was enough. Olympia needed nothing more.

"You're right, Laura, she's growing like a little weed. How's she doing with the day care?"

"She loves it. In the beginning she fussed a little, but now she's a regular part of the tribe. She wails when I pick her up."

Olympia chuckled. "You can't have it both ways, my girl. But tell me, how's the job going?"

"That's the least of my worries. I love it, and they seem to like me. The work is interesting, and I'm finally starting to make some friends."

"Guy friends, girlfriends, either or both?"

Olympia would never say it to her daughter, but she hoped in her heart that one day she'd find someone who would love her and include little Erica in that love.

"Mostly girlfriends," answered Laura with a characteristic toss of her hair. "The guys here at work are mostly married. There are a few singles around, but to be honest, I'm just not interested in a relationship with any of them, and I don't go out to bars. Never did. I'm still settling in. Don't go worrying about me, I'm okay."

"Good for you. Girlfriends are the best. They got me through the best of times and the worst of times." Olympia was watching the image on the screen and seeing Erica squirming and finally breaking free from her mother's arms.

"Well, that's the end of this conversation. She's on the loose, and that means I'm on my feet. Call me again when you can. It feels so good to talk to you."

"I will, honey. I'm glad you're making friends."

"I am, and if you come out again, maybe you'll meet some of them. I'd like you to—yikes, I gotta go." With a click and a bleep the screen went blank.

Olympia didn't know whether to laugh or cry, so she tried a little of each. Her daughter was okay. She was making friends. Friends are good. Friends are lifesavers. Olympia had Jim. He'd been her lifesaver more than once.

After that she tried her two sons, but neither of them responded. She left each of them messages, asking for good times to connect, and then tapped on the Skype icon for Jim. More bleeps and boops, and miracle of miracles, Jim's face appeared—with a beard!

"What the hell is that on your face?" Olympia dispensed with any formalities.

"What does it look like? I'm just trying it out; I never had one before. What do you think?"

"Now that I'm over the initial shock, it looks pretty good. Do you like it?"

"It will keep my face warm. It's freezing here. We actually had a few snowflakes over the weekend. It didn't stick around though, too early really."

"I love snow. I hope it holds off until I get back. How's your work going? Do you have a church yet?"

"Olympia, I've been an Episcopal priest for less than a month. I'm not even dry behind the ears yet. Let's just say I'm considering options, and so is the diocese."

"Is that a good or a bad thing?"

"It's a good thing. I'm not sure if I want a parish. I might want to go back to teaching. We'll see. What about you? What's happening over there? Have you solved the mystery yet?"

"Funny you should ask."

"Well, you did say you'd been invited over there to check out a problem situation."

"Hang on a minute, Jim. I'll be right back."

Olympia got up and closed the door to the internet room. What she was about to say to Jim was for his ears alone.

"That bad, is it?"

"How do you know?"

"I just watched you shut the door. That means whatever you are about to tell me does not want overhearing. Am I correct?"

"I wish you weren't, Jim. I need some advice, and I need some help."

"I'm listening."

Out in the garage Margery Mosley was checking on her husband's progress with the van. She'd passed Frederick going in the opposite direction, so she knew he'd be alone. She could see his feet and legs dangling out from beneath the driver's side door.

"How's it coming along, then?"

"It was just a fuse, but while I'm in here, I thought I'd check some of the other cables."

"What other cables are there? I'm surprised you can see anything in all that mess."

"Brakes, starter, alternator, battery … that's about it. They all connect to something or other."

"How can you tell one from the other?"

"You're full of questions today, aren't you, woman? I read the manual, then I cross my fingers that I've got the right one. Stick your head in here, and I'll show you."

Slowly, one by one, Robert lifted or pointed out the different cables and connectors and explained where they came from, what they connected to and what they did.

When he finished Margery said, "Hmph, interesting, not that I ever expect to be taking up car repair in my spare time, but I have to admit, I'm curious. You know me, I like to know how things work, always have."

"Aye, after thirty years I should know, but …" He stopped midsentence and changed direction. "What's all this about anyway? I don't think you've ever set foot in here before." If he had been going to say something else, he'd changed his mind.

"I came in to see if you've had y'lunch as well as to see if you've got the old thing running again. Then I got curious. I think that Olympia Brown woman might be asking if she can take it out one day."

"Aye, her husband said as much. Dead nuts for Volkswagens, she is, or so he tells me. She's got one of her own."

"So I've heard," said his wife. "And don't be bothered coming in, you'll only get grease everywhere. I'll bring you a bacon and chip butty and cup of tea, and you can have it out here, if y'd like."

"You're a good woman, Mrs. Mosely."

"Don't go spreading it about now, y'daft brush. I've got a reputation to maintain."

Olympia found Rosie in the sitting room, curled around a book.

"If this is a good time, we could go for that walk now. I've made my first Skype calls, and I need some fresh air to regain my equilibrium."

Rosie laughed. "That bad, was it?"

"No, actually, it was amazing. I got to see my daughter and my granddaughter."

"I thought you only had two sons."

"I probably told you I raised two sons. My daughter is another story, which I don't mind telling you, but it's you that wants a word with me, so I guess this walk is all yours."

"Thank you, Olympia. Let me run and get a jumper and the food I saved from breakfast. It looks a bit nippy out there."

She was back in minutes, and the two set off at a slow pace in the opposite direction from the pub and toward the old church where very recently Olympia had been sitting and talking with Celia Attison. They walked along, side by side, in silence. Olympia was leaving space for Rosie to open the conversation when and how she wished. There was indeed a chill in the air and a light breeze that ruffled Olympia's hair. She almost needed a hat but not quite. She was not as hardy as these English people seemed to be; maybe it was an acquired skill. Olympia was mentally going over her conversation with Celia when Rosie finally began to speak.

"I don't suppose you've noticed me sitting with Steve Warner," she asked.

"It would have been hard not to. You were the only two people in the sitting room when I went in there yesterday. Why, is—or was—something amiss? Should I have noticed something?"

"I'm in love with him, and he's in love with me, and he's married. The whole thing has me completely unsettled. You can't exactly plan these things."

"Oh, dear," said Olympia. She wasn't about to tell Rosie she'd been in that predicament herself once upon a time, but it did make her sympathetic to what she was hearing and the evident pain the woman was feeling.

Olympia considered putting her arm around Rosie but held back. This was England, and to all appearances people were much more reserved here. This was not the time to make a social blunder.

"Have you …?"

"No, at least not yet, anyway. But being here is one hell of a lot harder than I thought it was going to be. I'm a church lay leader, for God's sake. I'm not supposed to have affairs with married men, and look at me. I may not have gone to bed with him, but it's not for lack of opportunity or wanting to. We thought by coming here we would have time to talk and put it into some kind of perspective. It was a bad idea."

Olympia stopped walking and reached for Rosie's hand. To hell with etiquette. There was no amount of training that prepared anyone, clergy or not, for moments like this. Rosie needed another human being to be present to her pain, to listen and not pass judgment or offer advice, to neither encourage nor discourage, just listen and care. That she could and would do.

"Tell me about it, or rather, tell me what you want me to know and be assured you have my complete confidence."

Rosie's eyes expressed a gratitude that words could never do, and the two women continued on their walk.

"I suppose it started a few months ago. We kept meeting each other at various church functions and district events. We have a lot in common and enjoy one another's company—too much, unfortunately. One thing has not led to another, but being here together, away from our congregations and our families ..."

Olympia nodded sympathetically but said nothing.

"Damn damn damn!" Rosie stopped walking and began punching her right fist into the open palm of her left hand. "Damn, blast, shit, fuck, piss!"

"Double that and raise you five," said Olympia with a sad smile.

Rosie shook her head in frustration. "What the hell am I going to do, Olympia? My heart says go for it, my head tells me it's all wrong and I'm crazy. Ethically, I can't possibly let myself mess up a man's marriage, and at the same time my soul feels like it's being ripped in half."

Olympia winced at the painful and tragic image. She'd been there. She did understand.

"Maybe just talking about it, bringing all these feelings into the light, is a first step."

"What do you mean?"

"I mean the first step to finding any solution is to articulate the problem. Sometimes hearing the words coming out of your own mouth is a step toward coming to a decision."

"What would you do?"

Olympia decided this was not the time to tell her story. Maybe someday she would, but not now. "As I understand it, you have three points of view: your head, your heart and your soul. I don't know which of these is the strongest voice in how you live your life, but you do. This has become a painful situation for all concerned, and any decision either of you makes will likely cause even more pain before it gets better."

Rosie nodded miserably.

"People fall in love, Rosie. There's not much we can do about our feelings. Feelings are neither good nor bad, they just are. We only have control over how we act on those feelings. On one side of the argument, according to my grandmother anyway, if you have the courage to get yourself into a situation, then have just as much courage to keep your mouth shut and make sure nobody gets hurt. It's the old tree falling in the forest with no one to see it analogy. On the other side of the picture, my mother always used to say, if you don't like the heat, get out of the kitchen."

Rosie stopped walking and began rubbing her arms. She was shivering. "It's colder than I thought. I'm freezing. I think we should start back."

Olympia didn't need a hint. The discussion was over, and neither of them was interested in the food they'd taken along with them.

"Let's just leave it here for the birds and the beasties to find," said Olympia. "Might as well let it do some good."

When Olympia returned from her walk, she remembered her computer was still in the internet room. She was still experiencing the aftereffects of her cold, as well as feeling mentally exhausted. She was trying to decide whether to sit and numb out playing computer solitaire for a while or to skip the preliminaries and go straight off to her room and pass out. After a moment's hesitation her heavy eyelids and blurred vision made the decision for her, and in less than two minutes after she landed on her bed she was fast asleep.

Not five minutes later Frederick came into the room and found her. He smiled down at her, lifted the duvet from his own bed and tucked it around her before tiptoeing out of the room, careful not to let the door slam behind him.

Thus inspired by the sight of Olympia sleeping so peacefully, he decided to take up residence in a corner of the sitting room and do much the same. His plan was to start reading and then let nature take its course, which it inevitably would. The only other person in the room was Steve Warner, stretched out in a window seat in the corner, staring out of the window. Frederick could only hope, as he eased himself into the softest chair he could find, that he wouldn't snore too loudly and disturb the man's thoughts.

For the rest of the afternoon workshop members worked alone or in pairs. They struggled with their sermons, commiserated over cups of tea or went off on their own to think and write. Some followed Frederick's stellar example and took naps, and still others went off to the pub for a pint and a little fresh air. To the casual observer it was a typical day in a typical retreat agenda, only it wasn't. Below the well-ordered surface of the day-to-day schedule, several dark threads were twisting and turning and forming themselves into a deadly net. The question was, who or what was the intended victim?

Was Celia the target, or was it The Moorlands itself? He hadn't actually thought of that aspect, but why would someone want to do that? It was all very curious indeed, but … Frederick felt himself slipping into sleep. It was lovely.

Six thousand miles away in the company cafeteria, Laura Wiltstrom and a newfound friend, Gerry Adams, were seated across from each other, sharing a soup and salad lunch. Gerry had ordered the Greek salad special and Laura asked for the tomato, basil and fresh mozzarella baguette. Now they were doing their best to divide them evenly without too much landing on the table. It was a messy task, and the doing of it had the two of them in gales of laughter. Laura couldn't remember when she had last had this much fun and felt this happy. It made her wonder what was in the iced tea she was drinking. Was she finally beginning to settle in here? Certainly a tomato sandwich and Greek salad had never affected her this way before. She'd had so many years of feeling like a misfit, an outsider. Something was different here and now. Confidence, perhaps? Maybe California and this job and the people she was meeting were what had always been intended for her. Maturity sneaking in when she least expected it?

"Whatever it is, I'll take it."

"What did you just say?" asked Gerry.

"Nothing, really. I guess I was thinking out loud."

"Good thoughts, I hope," said Gerry.

"More than good; you must be a mind-reader. Let's eat. I'm starving."

Eighteen

The next morning a determined Celia stood in the doorway of Margery Mosely's office and waited until the dour woman looked up from her computer.

"Mrs. Mosely, I wonder if you could help me. I'm looking for something, and I don't know where to begin."

"What might that be? You may have noticed I'm rather busy right now, and I can't spare much time. You're the one who's been off sick, and I've had to do your work as well my own."

Celia smiled and nodded in dutiful acknowledgment. "I do appreciate it, Mrs. M. Now here's my question. I'm thinking about looking into our fluctuating attendance figures and doing a comparison study and graph of building use from the time The Moorlands was incorporated up to the present. Nothing about money, mind you, just overall use of the facility, numbers of guests, singles, couples and families, lengths of stays and seasonal trends. If I can learn when we get the most business and what kind of use is made of the place, maybe we can do more of what works so we can bring in more business. What do you think?"

"It will be some job of work, I'll tell you, and I have no time for it. That's what I think."

"I wasn't asking you to do it. I'll do it. I just need to know where I can find the old guest registers. We do have them, don't we?"

Margery looked away and began twisting a pencil between her fingers.

"Oh, we've got them, all right, and I know exactly where they are. It's more of a question of digging them out. That's what's going to take the time."

Celia couldn't tell whether the woman was looking wary or weary, but she refused to be put off and persisted.

"I can do that if you'll just tell me where they are. I really don't want to bother you."

"I've got all I can do to finish what's on my desk by the end of the day. If I finish by tea time, I'll take you up there, and you can help me pull out the boxes."

"Up there? Up where? Are they up in the attic then?"

"Everything's up in the attic, Mrs. Attison. My Robert hauled it all up there himself, and I stood there and told him where to put each and every box."

"I haven't actually been up there, but if you'll tell me where they might be, I'll get a torch and go find them myself. Then I won't be disturbing you any further."

She shook her head and waved her hand in the "halt" signal. "Oh, you shouldn't be going by there by yourself. Those boxes and cartons are piled up pretty high. If they started to fall, you could do yourself an injury. Why won't you just wait until this afternoon, and then I can get Robert to help? It really will be faster that way and certainly much safer."

Celia wondered if that was an implied threat. If it was, she was going to ignore it.

"Why don't you let me make that judgment, Mrs. M.? I'll go up there and see for myself. If it looks like more than I can handle, I'll come right back down. I don't think Richard is very busy. Maybe I could ask him to help me."

Margery was cornered and furious, and if she weren't in such near-perfect control of her emotions, it might have been obvious. All Celia could see was a tensing of her neck muscles and a tightening of her jaw.

"Don't say I didn't warn you."

In that moment, the gloves were off and on the floor between them. Each woman had a job to do, and neither knew the full extent of the other's will and determination to see the other fail, but they would soon find out.

Celia inclined her head in Margery's direction. "I stand warned, thank you. Now tell me which corner of the attic I might find the old registers. I'm assuming you've labeled the boxes."

"With contents and year."

"Please tell me where to find them, Mrs. Mosely."

Margery blew out a long breath and spoke her words slowly. "When you open the door at the top of the stairs, go to the left, over by t'window. I can't remember whether I stacked them with the oldest at the bottom or the top, so be careful."

The bloody hell you can't remember, thought Celia, who smiled most graciously at the glowering bookkeeper and said, "Oh, don't you worry, Mrs. M., I'll be most careful. Is it unlocked, or do I need a key?"

"We don't have a key, so we leave it unlocked. What's to steal? A load of old papers and some broken chamber pots? Who'd want that lot?"

The unspoken question hovered in the air between them. And what else, Mrs. Margery Mosely … and what else?

Sitting alone at her desk after Celia left the room, it was clear to Margery that her meticulously constructed plan was in real danger of coming undone. She needed to take immediate and decisive action and knew she could no longer include any of the others. They simply were not as invested in the outcome as she was. How could they be? They had no blood connection to any of this. And truly, when it came to the final act, the purchase and resale of The Moorlands, could she even trust her husband to follow through? He was too good hearted and might easily fall by the wayside. There was no way to go forward except on her own, and the sooner she got on with it the better.

She found Robert in the back garden, kneeling on the grass and mending a fence.

"There you are."

"What is it, Missus, you look a fright."

"I need a word."

"I'll be there in two shakes."

"This instant, Robert!"

He sighed heavily, put down his tools and stood to attention.

"When the fire alarm goes off, I need you to stay here for exactly five minutes, then come in by the rear door and meet me at the foot of the front staircase."

"Wha …?"

"Don't argue, man, just do as I say. I'll explain later. If I don't stop that woman right this minute, everything I've worked for these last thirty years could be lost. Now get back to your fence mending. Remember, when the alarm goes off don't say a word to any of the others. Just wait here, count out the minutes, and then get yourself to the staircase and wait for me there."

He looked taken aback by her feverish intensity. He'd only seen her like this twice before in the whole time they'd been married. The first was when the old lord of the manor died, and the second was when the board hired Celia Attison. Now was not the time to cross her. Robert knelt down by the fencepost, stared at his watch and waited for the sound of the fire alarm.

Upstairs in the old stone building, Celia Attison was starting up the last flight of stairs leading to the attic. The lighting, what there was of it, was dim and likely hadn't been upgraded since it was installed. She'd never been up here before, but she did know that besides storage rooms there were at least two bedrooms which in times of old had most likely been allotted to members of the domestic staff. She shivered and flicked on her torch so she could see the last few narrow stairs. The semi-central heating in the place stopped at the first floor. They couldn't afford to carry it any farther. Vents in the floors allowed some warmth to migrate upstairs to the guest bedrooms and bathrooms. This and great piles of heavy bedding kept people warm, at least mostly.

She pushed away the thought of expanding the central heating and continued plodding up the stairs as fragments of old Alfred Hitchcock horror films pushed their way into her thinking. This did nothing whatsoever for her sense of confidence. Attics and basements were the stuff of childhood fears and nightmares. She had never bothered to ask if this place had a ghost. Hmmm, another involuntary shiver.

Stop it, she scolded, it's a flight of stairs in an old building, and I've just reached the top. Now I am turning the handle and opening the door. She was talking herself through her nervousness, and it was almost working. The old besom downstairs said the boxes I'm looking for will be over by the window, which means there'll be some natural light up here. And there it is. Celia exhaled the breath she'd been hanging onto for dear life.

She pushed the creaky door open as far as it would go and started toward the window. As she did so the door slowly swung back into position and clicked shut behind her. The room where she was standing had to be one of the storage rooms. She could see two doors, one on either side, which must lead to the two bedrooms. I'll inspect those some other time she told herself.

The boxes stacked near the window were indeed labeled Guest Registers with the dates carefully lettered on the side facing out. "Okay so far," she said to the empty room. "That's number one. Now to see if I can find the account books. Aha! Would you believe? There they are, right beside the boxes of registers, boxes labeled accounts and their corresponding dates." Celia was pleased with herself.

She'd reached for the top one and started to lift it down so she could open it when the ear-splitting screech of the fire alarm sounded.

"What the hell?"

At first she told herself it had to be a false alarm, but false or not, as managing director she had no choice but to obey protocol and see that the guests and staff were all safely out of the building.

It was only when she reached for the doorknob that she realized there was no handle on the inside of the door, and she was locked in.

Nineteen

Downstairs in the empty dining room, Margery wedged three pieces of bread into the toaster on the sideboard, turned the dial up as far as it would go and pushed down the lever. She, too, was counting. When the smoke started frothing out of the toaster, she stood and waited until she saw flames. Only then did she walk out into the corridor, pull the fire alarm and wait patiently for all hell to break loose.

The guests were scattered about the property. Some were in the building, and others were out on the grounds. Frederick, with Steven Warner close on his heels, ran into the foyer, where they found Margery wide eyed with fear and trying to look in all directions at once. The two men spoke simultaneously over each other.

"What's happened?"

"Is this a fire drill?"

"Was it scheduled?"

Margery appeared to be completely undone. Her voice was shrill, and her hands were shaking.

"No, I'm afraid it's the real thing. There's smoke coming out of the dining room. I need to make sure everyone is out of the building before I go looking for it." She pointed toward the stairs. "Please, you two go up and knock on all the doors and see that everyone's out. I'll check the downstairs rooms. The alarm is connected to the nearest fire station, but it's all volunteer, so it will take a few minutes for them to get here.

"Oh, my God, Olympia's in the shower," yelled Frederick.

"No, I'm not." Her hair was still wet, but she was fully dressed and standing on the stairs behind him. "I need to run and get my laptop."

Frederick looked doubtful. "Well, then, hurry. There's smoke coming from the dining room, can you smell it? Get outside and wait for me there. I'll go and see to the others. Steve's gone up already. I won't be long."

As Olympia turned to go, Margery caught Frederick by the sleeve.

"Mr. Watkins, do you think you might go up to the top floor for me? I think Mrs. Attison might be trapped in there. She went up to get something just before the alarm sounded, and she didn't know the door won't open from the inside. Do hurry, the poor thing must be frightened out of her wits. How could I not have told her there was no handle …"

The rest of the sentence was lost in the mist as Frederick turned and raced up the stairs. As he did so, he could hear the pounding and Celia's frantic calls for help getting louder and louder.

"Hang on," he screamed over the alarm, "I'm coming."

When he reached the top he wrenched the door open, and Celia Attison raced past him and started down the stairs. The smell of smoke was getting stronger.

When the two reached the bottom, Margery told them to go outside and count heads, and she'd go make sure the kitchen staff was safely out.

"Got it all under control, haven't you, Margery?" Celia hissed the words under her breath. She was seething with rage and absolutely unable to do anything but follow instructions. Her first responsibility was to the guests, get them to safety, but where was Richard? Please, God, let him be outside.

"Celia?" Richard was calling from the doorway.

"I'm here. Oh, Richard!"

"Come outside, darling, I think we're all accounted for."

When everyone was safely out and standing around the front garden in worried clusters, Margery carefully and quietly locked the front entry door behind them and turned to greet her husband.

"We have less than ten minutes before the fire brigade gets here. I want you to go upstairs to the attic, take the three boxes marked Accounts, take them down by the back stairs and hide them in the wardrobe in our bedroom."

"But …"

"And while you're in there, make it look like someone's had a sort of dust-up there. Knock over one or two of the other boxes, spill out some of the contents and maybe break a chamber pot or a bit of bric-a-brac. Remember, our dear Celia was frightened and desperate to get out, and we have to make it look that way. Now get up the stairs."

Out in the front the conferees and staff were gathered, holding on to what few things they could carry. They were relatively calm because of Celia, who was now back and fully in charge. As she pointed out, there were no flames leaping out of windows and the smoke was not billowing from anywhere she could see. "Very likely it was a frayed wire or something burning in the kitchen. We'll know soon, but we are staying here until we do. I hope you aren't getting too cold."

"Celia, have you or anyone else seen Rosie Lewis? She's not here. She's not still inside, is she?" Richard Attison had just realized they were missing one of their group members."

"She's gone," said Steve Warner.

"Are you sure of that?"

He nodded and held up a piece of paper. "She's packed up and left. I found this on her bed. All it says is she had an emergency and had to leave. She apologizes for not telling anyone, but there was no one about. We are not to worry. She says she's fine, and she'll send a message when she gets home." Steve crumpled the paper, jammed it in his pocket and turned away just as the sounds of sirens could be heard approaching from the direction of the village.

Later that day, when the firemen and their noisy trucks had departed, the staff and guests were all sitting together in the dining room, cradling cups of hot tea. Celia stood and called for their attention.

"First, let me thank you all for your splendid behavior, your quick response and your readiness to do whatever was needed. I am profoundly grateful that our fire scare was nothing more than an unattended toaster, but we all know it could have been much worse. I particularly want to thank Mrs. Mosely for acting so responsibly in my untimely absence. Who would have thought I could have been so stupid as to lock myself in the attic? I might add that first on the to-do list for tomorrow will be to put a new handle on the inside of that door."

"I love to fix doorknobs, especially broken ones. I'll do that for you." It was Frederick being helpful, slightly ridiculous and most endearing. It made people laugh and lifted their collective moods.

Olympia shook her head and smiled. Trust Frederick to break the tension, she thought, but it's going to take more than a new doorknob to fix the tension in this place. Then her thoughts wandered to Steven Warner. She looked around the room to where he might be sitting, but he was nowhere to be seen. Best leave him alone, she thought, but keep an eye out for him, as well.

Around her people were putting their cups and saucers onto the tea trolley and slowly getting themselves back on the job. The excitement was over, and so was the tea break; it was time to get back to work.

"Olympia, do you have a few minutes? I need to go back up to the attic, and I want someone to hold the door open for me." It was Celia.

"It's no wonder after what just happened. I don't think I'd set foot up there again without a bodyguard and a locksmith. That must have scared the hell out of you."

"Oh, that it did, but I'm fine now, and I need to get back up there as soon as possible." She dropped her voice to a whisper. "I found what I was looking for. I found the early accounts books. I had to leave them there when I thought I was running for my life. Now that I'm not, I need to go back and get them."

"Do you want to do it right now?"

"If you don't mind."

"Okay, then."

Standing in the corner of the room while finishing the last of her tea, Margery watched the two women leave. She was nodding her head and smiling. She was back on track.

In the kitchen Mrs. Loring, the cook, was back in her domain and once again queen of all she surveyed. With her composure now fully regained, she went about discarding the charred toaster and replacing it with a new one fresh out of the box. Then she posted a dire warning to all and sundry about the dangers of over filling the toaster and, worse still, leaving it unattended.

Margery returned to her office, locked the door and powered up her computer. There were a few things she needed to move for safekeeping, and she couldn't risk being interrupted.

Twenty

While Olympia and Celia were making their way up the attic stairs, the rest of the members of the conference, minus Rosie Lewis and Frederick, who had taken himself off to the pub, were gathered in the sitting room. On a low table in the center of the circle was an open bottle of sherry and a bowl of crisps. Gillian Steele and Janet Lofton were sitting close to the fire, surrounded by what looked like miles of yarn. They discovered they had a common interest in knitting, and whenever time permitted, out came the needles.

Vaughn Weller and Richard Attison were in another corner discussing the merits of extemporaneous speaking as compared to reading sermons from a written script. Steve Warner was seated a little apart from the others, holding a tumbler full of sherry. It was a convivial group. They'd all had a bit of a scare, and now they were relaxing and coming back into focus—all of them except Steve, who remained hunched over his glass, looking at the floor and sipping his wine. If any of them wondered about the cause of his somber appearance, he or she was careful not to ask. It was clear the man needed some space.

Both Celia and Olympia were carrying their torches as they mounted the stairs to the attic. The creaks and squeaks of the old, tired treads beneath their feet added to the general creepiness of their task. Olympia was mortified to find herself short of breath as they neared the top and decided that if anyone asked, she would blame the dust.

Celia pushed open the door and gasped.

"What's wrong?"

"Someone's been up here."

What are you talking about? We all had to go outside when the alarm sounded. Nobody's been up here."

Celia stepped into the room and moved off to the side. "See for yourself. I didn't leave it like this. There was nothing out of place when I came downstairs. "

Olympia clapped her hand to her open mouth. She was about to shout, "Holy shit" but instantly thought better of it. "What the …"

"Hell," finished Celia.

Before either of them said or did anything further, Olympia dragged a box over to the door and propped it open. The room before them had clearly been disturbed. A box of books been overturned, there was a broken chamber pot in the middle of the mess, and some papers had been scattered across the floor. Celia looked for the boxes of account books, but it didn't take her long to discover they were no longer there.

"That old witch," hissed Celia. "Somehow, she—or someone—managed to get up here while we were all outside and make off with the boxes containing the account books."

"What are you talking about?" Olympia was looking around and doing her own mental calculations.

Celia turned and faced her, steely eyed. "When I was up here before I saw three boxes labeled Accounts. They're not here now; someone's taken them."

"You're sure you're not imagining you saw them or something that looked like it might be them?" Olympia immediately regretted her words.

"It may have been dim in here, Olympia, but I know what I saw and what I didn't see. The boxes are gone."

Olympia was immediately and justly contrite. "I'm sorry for saying that, Celia. This has been a trying afternoon for all of us. I guess I was wondering if you mistook one thing for another in all the confusion when you were locked in and couldn't get out. I apologize."

"And I apologize for snapping at you. We're all under a strain."

"What now?"

Celia lifted her chin. "I'm marching myself right downstairs and, uh …"

"What?"

In a flash Celia's look of defiance turned to defeat. "Damn. I don't know what to do. Who do I ask? What do I say?"

"I've got an idea," said Olympia.

"I'm glad you do."

"Look, someone, and we both suspect it's Mrs. Mosely, is waiting for you to come screaming downstairs with your hair on fire."

"Do you mind using another metaphor?"

"Oops, sorry about that."

They both chuckled, and Olympia began again. "What I'm suggesting is that you say absolutely nothing, give her no reaction whatsoever, nada. It will drive her batty. Then just sit back and see how she reacts. It could be interesting. Meanwhile, I'm supposed to go have a chat with the cook sometime before Friday. She's going to give me her sticky toffee pudding recipe."

"You're joking. How did you manage to get on that one's good side in less than four days?"

"Flattery. It's gets you anywhere. And while I'm in there with her, I'll see what else I can stir up, pun intended. It's an apology for the hair joke."

"Hair today and gone tomorrow," quipped Celia, who was clearly beginning to feel better.

"Okay, so mum's the word for now. Let's first clean this place back up so it looks like did the first time you were here. Then we each take a box of the old registers with us and get the hell out of here."

"What good will that do?"

"Someone is trying to discredit you and make you look incompetent, Celia. If you go back down acting like nothing's happened, at some point she's going to come up here and see for herself. She could have created the mess herself during the fracas with the fire alarm, but more likely she made her poor husband do it while she stood guard at the bottom of the stairs."

"It all makes sense, doesn't it? I wish it didn't."

"I suspect we're all going to know before long. Meanwhile, let's do it and get out of here. This place is starting to give me the creeps. Has anyone said anything about spirits up here?"

"Not in my hearing, but I was wondering about the same thing myself when I came up here the first time. It sort of feels like it, doesn't it?"

Maybe I should ask Miss Winslow if she has any opinion on the matter, thought Olympia, an idea which for the moment she wisely decided not to share with Celia.

"I think we have enough to uncover right now without adding any of the dearly departed to the mix, wouldn't you say?"

"I say, let battle commence."

When the two of them had finished restoring the room to order, Olympia pushed away the box holding the door and started down the dark narrow stairs. Behind them the door slowly creaked itself shut.

When they reached the ground floor, Margery was nowhere in sight. The two women carried their boxes into Celia's office and set them on the floor of the coat closet.

Celia dusted off her hands and turned towards Olympia. "Now what?"

"Keep calm and carry on. Isn't that what you people say over here? I suggest you go back to business as usual, as much as that is possible. Say nothing, and wait for her to make the first move. It will totally unhinge her. She's expecting explosives, and you are handing her warm milk. It should be interesting, but be careful."

"What do you mean?"

Olympia hesitated before she responded. "Celia, there is something very unhealthy about that woman. I wish I could be more specific. I have the feeling that if cornered, she could be dangerous. I repeat, be careful. In more ways than one, you could be playing with fire here. Don't let it get out of control."

"Not a comforting thought, Olympia."

"It wasn't intended to be, but I need to get back to the group. They are supposed to be working on sermons, but somehow I think they may have been sidetracked."

"Thank you for all of this, Olympia. I'm beginning to understand why Richard thinks so highly of you and why he invited you here."

"Let's just call it a situation of fortuitous convergence of parallel cognition."

"Could you say that again in English?"

Olympia grinned. "Great minds run on the same track."

Margery Mosely was kneeling in front of the fire in her cottage sitting room. She was tearing page after page out of the account books and carefully feeding them into the flames. The heat was warming the skin on her face, flushing it pink and then scarlet as she continued with her task. She was breathing heavily with the effort of it all, but she had no choice. It had to be done now. She kept perfect accounts of everything. It was no more than what was expected of her, and it was what she expected— no, demanded—of herself. She smiled as she held out another page to the flame. Let them try and find anything now. Good luck to them.

On the way to the sitting room Olympia detoured through the kitchen to see if she could find Mrs. Loring. Not surprisingly, she was standing by the Aga.

"Oh, there you are. I was planning to come to see you earlier this afternoon, but things got a bit out of hand."

"Not half."

"Is there a time I might drop by tomorrow. I am *not* going back to the States without that recipe."

"I usually take my elevenses in the room back there," she pointed with the spoon she was holding. "How about half eleven, then?"

"I'll be there. Thank you."

"If you want a biscuit, I just set some fresh ones over on the sideboard. They might still be warm."

Olympia thanked her and helped herself to not one, but two. They were still warm, and the smell was intoxicating. It had been a long day, and biscuits, or cookies as she was used to calling them, had the power to soothe and refresh. She glanced over her shoulder to see if the cook was watching, grabbed a third and sprinted out of the room.

Twenty-One

On the way back to her office Margery poked her head through Celia's door, ostensibly to see if she was all right and thank her for her kind words earlier that day. Celia looked up from the papers on her desk and smiled.

"Think nothing of it, Mrs. M. You stepped in when I wasn't able to. That's what makes things work around here. We're supposed to be a team, don't you agree?" She paused, looking at the woman in the doorway. Margery looked as if she was trying to say something. Celia was the very picture of wide-eyed innocence.

"Um, did you find what you were looking for when you went upstairs, the boxes with the old registers, I mean?"

"As a matter of fact I did. They were right where you said they'd be. No need to take them down now that I know where they are. They won't be going anywhere, will they?"

"Everything's all right up there then?" The woman was the very picture of sly innocence.

"Why on earth wouldn't it be? You oversee the storing of things, and the attic was as well ordered as you keep your desk. I was very impressed."

"Nothing out of order?"

Celia balled her hands into fists under the desk to keep from laughing out loud. If the implications and ramifications of all of this subterfuge weren't so dire, this would be like something out of Gilbert and Sullivan, only she knew it wasn't.

"Nothing that I could see, but then what do I know? Aren't you the one that oversees the record keeping and the storage of same? I'm new here, Mrs. Mosely. You're the one with the history."

Margery looked like she had a hot potato in her mouth and wanted to spit it out, but instead she lifted her chin and said, "Very well, then I'll be off now."

When she left Celia turned back to her own work and noticed a small plate with three iced biscuits on it, which someone had left on her desk while she was out of the office. She automatically reached for one and was about to bite into it when she remembered Olympia's warning about eating anything she hadn't prepared herself. Then she thought about everyone drinking their tea out of the same pot earlier in the day. Had that been a mistake? Too late now; she had no option but to wait and see. It had been several hours since she'd had the tea and, fingers crossed, so far, so good. Celia took one of the biscuits, wrapped it in a paper napkin and slipped it into a side pouch on her purse.

She leaned forward, propped her elbows on edge of the desk and dropped her head into her hands. Maybe, when all of this was settled, she would look for another job. She'd been hired to turn The Moorlands around and make it a viable operation, but it would seem that someone was trying to do the exact opposite and make sure it failed. Why would anyone want to do that, or to be more accurate, why is *she* doing that?

Celia lifted her head, took a deep breath and smiled as a possible answer occurred to her: because someone might have a lot to gain if it fails, like a lot of hidden money. Her racing thoughts were interrupted by the repeated clang of the dinner bell and the memory of Olympia's warning. Don't eat anything here. It was time to find her husband and tell him she was going home a little early. No, she wasn't feeling poorly, in fact just the opposite. It had been a long day, and she was hungry. She didn't tell her husband the real reason she was going home early. Celia was planning to call the members of the board and request an emergency meeting as soon as possible.

With things inside The Moorlands apparently back to
normal, Frederick went back to the pub on a mission of his own.
He'd timed his arrival to be when business would be light, and
he could chat with the barman and not interfere with the man's
work. It had been a productive afternoon. Frederick had learned
a lot about the history of the village and even more about the
history of Margery Mosely. Now it was already dark and time to
go back to The Moorlands and tell the Attisons and Olympia
what he'd learned.

The way was familiar to him now, and he was striding along
as though he lived there when he saw a man stagger and fall on
the road ahead of him. Without a second thought Frederick
rushed to help and discovered it was Steven Warner sprawled at
his feet. One look and one whiff told him the man was drunk as a
most unprepossessing and disheveled lord.

Frederick leaned over, got his two hands under the man's
armpits and dragged him off to the side of the road out of harm's
way. Now what to do? The man was a sight, a sight no one
should see and one poor Warner would likely prefer not to
remember. On the other hand, considering the condition of the
man at his feet, he was not likely to remember anything. Warner
was curled on the ground, snoring wetly against the brick
sidewalk.

It was about ten minutes' walk from The Moorlands, and by
the look of him, the man on the ground wasn't going anywhere.
He'd go back and find Robert Mosely and ask him to help. No
point in alerting the others and causing the poor bloke even more
embarrassment when he sobered up.

As Frederick picked up his walk to an even trot, he
wondered where they could keep Warner hidden until he came
round. Something else to ask Robert Mosely, he told himself,
and I wonder where I might find him at this hour?

Robert, Margery and Thomas, the cat, were all sitting by the fire having their tea when Frederick knocked on the door.

"Door's open," called Margery.

Frederick entered and stopped just past the threshold.

"Um, Robert, I wonder if you might be able to lend me some assistance. I've got a bit a problem out here that needs another pair of man's hands."

"What might that be, Mr. Watkins?" Margery looked sharp-eyed and suspicious.

"We have a bit of an awkward situation outside, Mrs. M. One of the punters has had too much to drink and needs a little help getting up to his room. I think he'd rather the others didn't see him like this so I thought …"

"Go on then, Robert, take him up the back stairs. It's your Christian duty. And take an extra jumper so you don't catch a chill." Margery waved him off like an irksome fly and returned to staring at the fire and sipping her tea.

When the two men were outside, Frederick said, "I don't suppose you've got a wheelbarrow?"

"Is he that bad, then?"

Frederick grimaced and nodded. "Pissed as a newt."

Warner was right where Frederick had left him and floppy as a smelly ragdoll as they tried to maneuver him onto the barrow.

"We'll do as Margery suggested and take him 'round to the rear and up the back staircase."

"I didn't know there was another stairway."

Mosely nodded. "Aye, there's a total of three, if you're counting. This is the second back one. It's not like we are trying to hide it; we just don't use this one very much. They're marked as fire exits, but originally they were for the servants to use. They go all the way to the top of the house. Couldn't have the servants going up to bed where the lord and lady of the manor might see 'em, now could we?" He snorted. "What rubbish. I'm glad those days are gone."

He started to say something else but stopped just as they wheeled the barrow and Steven up to the door. He was starting to stir.

"Up we go, my friend," said Frederick.

He positioned himself on one side, and Robert took the other, and between them they managed to haul the poor man up the stairs and into his room without anyone being the wiser.

Frederick wet the corner of a towel and wiped the Steven's face and neck, and the two of them pulled off his shoes. Mosely thoughtfully put the tin wastebasket next to the bed and then went back and got a glass of water and left it within reach on the nightstand. Then the two of them left the way they came, quietly, down the back stairs. When they were outside once again, Robert shook his head.

"That man is not going to be very happy tomorrow morning, poor bugger."

"I don't think he's very happy right now, which likely explains why he's in the condition he's in."

"Happens," said Mosely.

"To the best of us," said Frederick.

"Cold orange juice and plenty of Paracetemol."

Frederick nodded. "It'll either kill him or cure him, but either way, I'll see that he gets it."

When Frederick joined the others at dinner, they were already well into their pudding, and there was not time to tell Olympia what he'd learned in the pub. He wanted to speak to her first and get her thoughts on what to tell who and when to do it, and that would require some time alone. Of course, time alone with Olympia often led to other things. He smiled. Control yourself, Watkins, all in due time. No, I take that back, we are leaving on Friday; that give us only two days. Priorities, man. Crikey!

Olympia was playing catch-up that night. The events of the day had interrupted her workshop schedule, so that evening they agreed to have a sermon session in the sitting room by the fire. Frederick planned to park himself in a corner with a book and wait until such time as he might have a word with his lady wife.

The opportunity came later when the two were sitting chastely in their separate beds, each with a cup of chamomile tea. When he finished the saga, Olympia whistled and shook her head in amazement.

"That is some tale. Who'd have thought?

"Precisely. Who in the world would remember the poor disgraced kitchen maid, and even if they did, how likely is it that person would know anything about her granddaughter?" said Frederick.

"I'm still trying to get my head around it. It happened almost seventy years ago."

"Who knows why people do what they do, Olympia. We'll never know what Margery's mother told her or what really happened. It's all hearsay history now. That's some grudge to be carrying."

"We can't make assumptions, Frederick. If, in fact, Margery Mosely is the one who is bankrupting this place, it would be nice to find out why."

"Revenge, most likely, and I don't think there anything nice about it."

"Wrong word, sorry, Frederick. So is it revenge or some sort of vendetta, or is it simple greed with no personal history at all? The woman is very smart, she's very good with numbers. She saw an opportunity and seized it. If the story is true, then she was probably dirt poor as a child, and now she sees a chance to be rich and the devil take the hindmost. It could be as simple as that."

"It could be, but I don't think it is."

"I wish I didn't agree with you, Frederick. That woman is strange. There's something about her. I've been watching. There are times when I've seen her just stop wherever she is and start staring into space at nothing—well, nothing I can see. Next she starts pulling at her collar. Then it's like she snaps back into the here and now and just carries on like nothing happened. Weird, I'll tell you."

"We have to tell Richard and Celia first thing in the morning."

"It's late, darling, and we've both had a long day."

"By the way, Steven Warner was missing tonight. You didn't happen to see him while you were out, did you? He was looking pretty rough this afternoon after he got word that Rosie left."

"He's safe in bed."

"How do you know?"

"Because Robert Mosely and I dragged him upstairs and poured him into it. He went and got himself thoroughly and completely paralytic with drink. He's sleeping it off."

"Oh, dear," said Olympia.

"It's late, darling, and we've both had a long day."

"You said that before."

"You didn't hear me the first time."

Twenty-Two

On Thursday morning the retreat was moving into high gear as well as closure mode. When they gathered in the conference room on that next to last morning, Richard asked each of them to write up the most significant points of the week with an eye to publishing. He said he envisioned either an article or part of a book. He asked them to work in dyads in the morning, and after lunch he planned for them to meet and pull it all together. He was feeling good. Despite staff tensions and low morale, a couple of broken hearts and a false fire alarm, they'd managed to accomplish something meaningful.

When the week ended, each of them would go back to their homes and congregations and write up their own section of the project. Then and he and Olympia would edit it and get it into production—at least, that was the plan. Yes, he told himself, it has been and still is, by God, a good week.

Steven Warner, hollow eyed and pale, was back among them, but he was clearly unwell. Still, he soldiered on, making the best of what was left of the week. Only Frederick and Olympia knew the double truth behind his malaise and compassionately said nothing to anyone. Hadn't Olympia had a dreadful cold earlier in the week? He'd probably caught it from her.

Margery was again in her office with the door locked. One of the members of the board, sympathetic to the side of tradition and opposed to any sort of change, rang to tell her that Celia had called an executive meeting of the board, something to do with an irregularity in the accounting. Margery was literally quivering with rage and fear. There was only one course of action left. She heard Celia enter the office next door. There might still be time. She picked up the phone and tapped the intercom button.

"Good morning, Mrs. Attison. I wonder if I might ask you for a bit of help this morning? Before you arrived, cook came in to tell me she's ordered some supplies that need picking up at a supplier up in Ripon. Ordinarily Robert would do it, but he's gone off in our car in the opposite direction. I don't want to ask old Bud Loring. His eyesight's not what it used to be for driving that far alone."

This is not what I need, thought Celia. On the other hand, today, more than ever, I must carry on and act as if nothing is amiss.

"Let me think about it. When does she need them by?"

"It's for the farewell dinner tonight. She can't leave the kitchen, and she can't spare any of the girls. I already asked. You know there's always a special supper the last night of a retreat. She'll be in a total swivet by now. I daren't go near her."

Celia groaned inwardly. "Let me see if I can get someone. Maybe if Frederick isn't busy I can ask him. He knows how to drive over here."

"Oh, um, he might not be able to find things. You know men can't find anything in grocery stores. Why, my Robert is absolutely hopeless when it comes to shopping. Are you sure you can't find a way to do it yourself?"

"Let me see if I can find Frederick. If I can't, I'll do it."

"Do let me know," asked Margery. "I don't want to be worrying about it."

"Of course, Mrs. M. I'll go and see to it right now."

Celia reluctantly got up from her own desk and went off in search of Frederick.

Olympia, she knew, would be with the workshop people, but would Frederick be there as well?

She poked her head through the door of the sitting room, but Frederick was not there. Olympia looked up, and Celia caught her eye and beckoned her to come out into the hallway.

"Is Frederick available?"

Olympia looked doubtful. "I don't think so. He said since the light was so beautiful this morning, he thought he'd go out with his camera. He may not even be back for lunch. Once he's out, he's out. There's no telling when we'll see him."

"Damn!"

"What was that?"

"I said, damn. The cook needs something at one of the wholesalers on the other side of Ripon, and it's almost an hour from here. She's asked me to go, but it will absolutely kill my morning."

She lowered her voice. "I've been on the phone with the board."

"What happened? What did you say, what did they say?" Olympia was all ears.

"The short answer is, I've called a meeting for tomorrow afternoon, and then who knows what will happen? I'm glad you'll still be here."

Olympia brightened. "I know what; I can take the old van. I'd suggest borrowing your car, but I'm more used to driving VWs. If you'll give me directions ..."

Celia shook her head. "I don't think so. You might be comfortable driving a van, Olympia, but you're not used to driving on the left. Can't have you cracking yourself up, now can we, and my car's not insured for a third driver. Damn!" Celia was beaten. "Okay, plan C. I take my car, and you come along with me, and I can tell you what the board said.

And I can tell you what Frederick learned about Margery Mosely with no one around to hear, thought Olympia, and one more piece of this puzzle slips into place.

When Celia went back to tell Mrs. Mosely that she'd be able to do the errand after all, she was not prepared for her response.

"You'll need to take the van. I neglected to tell you it's a big order, too big for a passenger car. But not to worry, Robert was out there working on it just yesterday; it's running like a little top, it is."

When Celia went back to tell Olympia the good news, her face lit up like the proverbial Christmas tree. "Yippee! Can I drive it, even just a little way? Not in town but around here where there's not too much traffic? I've been dying to drive over here, but Frederick wouldn't let me."

"Right! Where the locals drive like maniacs and the roads twist and turn like knotted ropes? Not a good idea."

Olympia dropped to her knees and clasped her hands to her chest."Pleeeaase," she whined.

Celia laughed and threw up her hands. "Oh, all right. I don't suppose there will be a problem so long as I'm in the car with you. We are insured for extra drivers in that one."

"When do we leave?"

"I need to tell Richard and Mrs. Loring, so let's say in about ten minutes."

Safely inside her office, Margery was smiling. Everything was almost back on track. This was not exactly how she'd originally planned things, but in the end she knew justice would finally be served. She looked at the closed door and then at the clock. It was time to notify the bank.

Olympia was all but jumping up and down like a little kid. She'd been wanting to try her hand at driving here. Now not only would she be driving on the left, but she'd be doing it in an almost historic—well, at least vintage—VW van. It was a dream come true. She missed her beloved van almost as much as she missed her cats. Maybe it was time to go home. The trials and tribulations of The Moorlands and its surrounds faded into the mist as she clambered up into the passenger seat.

"Seat belts," said Celia, twisting around and fastening her own.

"I didn't know cars this old had them."

"We had them installed. Health and Safety. If employees are going to drive it, we are required to have them."

"When can I have a go?"

"Keep your knickers on, woman, let me get it out of here and up the road a little way first. The view is much prettier, I thought you might as well enjoy that, as well."

As they pulled away Olympia listened to the signature clattery rattle of a VW engine in full throttle. She knew it well. It was music to her ears, but it was the three-hundred-sixty degree view that most fully captured her attention. The scenery around them was staggering. As far as Olympia could see there were rolling hills divided into quilt-shaped pieces by the stone walls that crisscrossed the hills and dales. First on one side of the road and then the other in a continuous, interweaving pattern of lines and shapes, the landscape rose to meet them and then fell away in sheer drops unimpeded by guard rails of any kind. This did not inspire confidence. She didn't remember such precipitous drops from the drive here on the previous Friday. Oh, well, never mind, Celia's used to it.

It wasn't long before Celia signaled and pulled off to the left. Olympia flinched involuntarily. She still wasn't used to which side was which and knew she would need to be fully attentive when behind the wheel. The two women switched seats and rebuckled themselves securely into place. Olympia sat for a moment, and then she put her foot on the clutch and pressed it to the floor. After that she walked herself through the gears and tested the brakes foot and hand. When she felt confident about where things were she shifted into first gear, signaled right, eased back on to the road. Once they were moving steadily forward, she worked through the gears and carefully steered to

the left side of the faded yellow line. The steering was a little
loose, and the brakes were a bit on the low side, but this could be
expected in such an old vehicle.

The road ahead was narrow, and it seemed to be forever
turning off in one direction and then right back on itself fifty feet
later. Fortunately, there was very little oncoming traffic, and
anything she could see in the rearview mirror was at a
comfortable distance. Olympia was feeling more confident by
the minute. I can do this, she thought—piece of cake!

Then Celia threw up her hands and screamed.

"Jesus Christ, Olympia, look out."

Cresting the hill and barreling toward them was a massive
transport lorry. Because the road was narrow, the vehicle was
well over the center line, leaving them no room to pass.

Olympia gasped and reacted instinctively, American that she
was. She wrenched the steering wheel to the right and slammed
her foot on the brake pedal, smashing it all the way to the floor
with no response whatsoever. No brakes! The van continued
crazily forward and to the right over the center line.

The last thing she heard was the sound of an air horn,
screeching brakes and breaking glass. The last thing she saw was
all that lovely scenery with the sheep and the stone walls and the
great puffy clouds building in the west all spinning around and
around and around.

Twenty-Three

Margery was enjoying a cup of tea and a second biscuit with Mrs. Loring when the phone call came. Moments later Richard Attison came tearing into the kitchen with tears streaming down his face. "There's been an accident, but thank God they're going to be all right."

Margery clutched at her throat. "What are you saying? Oh, God, tell me it isn't true."

"No, no, Mrs. M. You don't understand. There's been an accident, but my wife and Olympia are going to be okay. Celia just called. She wants me to come and get them."

"Margery, what's the matter? You've gone all peelie-wally. I don't think you heard right. They're not hurt. They're coming back. Do you need another cup of tea?" Mrs. Loring was on her feet now, hovering over the bookkeeper, who indeed had gone a sickly shade of grey.

Margery straightened up in her chair and took a deep breath. "It's just the shock of hearing it, that's all. I'll be all right. I just need a few minutes for my heart to stop racing." And then to emphasize it, she patted her chest and took a couple of deep breaths. "There, I feel better already."

In San Jose, California, Olympia's daughter, Laura Wiltstrom, was doing her best to set the table for dinner. She was high-stepping over and around little Erica, who was chasing after her yelling, "Me-do, mama, me-do," at top volume. She pushed her hair back and handed two spoons to the little girl and bought herself a one minute respite from the din. Why do they always do this? Laura was having her first guest for dinner, and she felt like a teenager going to her first dance. But why on earth was that? Gerry was a sweetheart and totally easy going. She wouldn't care if the plates matched or the fork was on the right side or the left and whether the napkins were paper or linen.

Earlier that week Laura had finally decided it was time she started entertaining, and Gerry seemed like the logical choice of a first real guest. They were near the same age, had several interests in common, and Laura felt ready to open her doors to someone besides herself and her daughter. Didn't Gerry say she liked children? Would Erica pass muster? Why the hell was she so worried about what Gerry thought? Not worried, nervous. So what was there to be nervous about? Nervous that she might not measure up? Measure up to what? Who's counting?

Laura's internal wrangle was interrupted by the sound of the doorbell. She whipped off her apron, smoothed her hair and went to answer it. When she pulled open the door, Gerry was standing outside with an armload of brilliant yellow chrysanthemums.

"Wow, "said Laura.

"My mother told me always to bring a hostess gift when you went to somebody's house. You wouldn't let me bring food, so I brought these."

"They're beautiful, thank you."

"I hope you like yellow."

"I like yellow, and I love chrysanthemums. They are one of my favorite flowers. The smell of them almost makes me homesick for New England. It's sort of crispy and spicy all at the same time."

"Uh, Laura?"

"What?"

"Can I come in now, or are you planning to have supper out here?"

Richard Attison was standing in the front entry when Frederick returned to The Moorlands.

"What have we here, a welcoming committee of one?" Frederick was all smiles as he walked up the path. He'd had a good day.

"I think you'd better come in and sit down, Frederick. There's been an accident. Celia and Olympia took the old van to pick up some supplies in Ripon, and they went off the road. "

Frederick blanched, but before he could speak, Richard held up his hand and continued.

"No, it's not what you think. They're both going to be all right. Badly shaken up, a few cuts and bruises, and the van's a total loss, but they were both belted in when it rolled over, and the police found them. Thank God they weren't hurt."

"Where are they now?" Frederick seemed to have lost control of his voice as well of his legs. It was shaking just as badly as the rest of him.

"They're waiting at the local hospital, expecting to be picked up. I didn't want to leave until you got back; that way I could take you with me. I knew you'd want to see them as soon as you could. "

"When did you find out?"

"The police called about an hour ago. They said they aren't sure exactly what happened yet, but they did say it was the American woman who was driving."

"Bloody hell," said Frederick. He was beginning to regain his color.

"When the police and the ambulance got there, they were both hanging upside down in their seatbelts, shaken up but completely intact. I hate to think what might have happened."

"Don't say it," snapped Frederick. "Let's just get there. I want to see my wife."

"Right-o," said Richard, "I'm parked in front."

Inside the building Margery was talking on the phone to her doctor. "That's correct. So I can come in tomorrow morning. Right. I'll be there. Thank you, I appreciate your finding time to see me."

She hung up the phone and sat in her chair, looking around the office she'd worked in for the best part of the last thirty years. Would she miss it? Would she miss all that The Moorlands had become to her? Certainly not the people; they meant nothing to her. Robert? What about him? But then she wouldn't be missing him, would she?

Margery had just set Plan B into motion, but she was the only one who knew. She had always had a Plan B. It was the only way she could do what she felt she must. Margery Mosely did not, could not, make mistakes.

Richard Attison was clutching the wheel with both hands and driving at or above the speed limit and Frederick, seasoned English driver that he was, found himself periodically gasping and covering his eyes. In less than an hour they pulled into the visitor parking area, and five minutes after that they were sitting in adjoining cubicles with their bruised but bravely smiling wives.

Olympia had a nasty black left eye and a rather large plaster on her forehead over the right eye. Those, a brace for her sprained wrist and the promise of one hell of a headache and stiff neck for the next couple of days were the extent of her injuries.

Celia appeared to be more shaken and disoriented than Olympia, but she too sported only a couple a cuts from flying glass, a rather large purple lump on her forehead and, of all things, a twisted ankle. There were two wooden crutches leaning on the wall beside the bed with the name Attison written in black marker along the edge.

Both men were in tears, and both women were trying to reassure them that they really were okay, honest, and could they please go home now.

Once they were in the car Olympia and Celia did their best to relate what happened, but even they were fuzzy on the details. As it turned out, Olympia's reflex lunge to the right is what probably saved their lives. The truck was so far out of its lane that if she had pulled left, they would have crashed. They rolled over because once the van was on the other side of the road, there was nowhere to go but up the embankment, and given the center of gravity in the van, there was nowhere to go after that but over … and over again.

"Thank God for those seatbelts," said Celia.

"Wait a minute,"

"What it is, love?" Frederick could not keep from stroking her hands and rubbing her back as she curled against him in the rear seat. He was still weak with relief.

"I remember something else. When I put my foot on the brake, nothing happened."

"That probably helped save you as well," said Richard.

"Hang on," said Frederick. "You stepped on the brake, and nothing happened?"

"The brakes were working when I was driving it," said Celia.

"And they were working, or at least I got resistance, when I stepped on them before I took the wheel," said Olympia.

"Do either of you know where they towed the van?" asked Frederick.

"The police will know, but what good will that do? It's a total loss." Richard had the steering wheel of Celia's Fiesta in a strangle hold, and he wasn't letting go.

"First the brakes worked, then they didn't. Does that tell you anything?"

"It's an old car. Things break down all the time," said Richard.

"But Robert Mosely was out working on it just yesterday, and Margery told me this morning that it was running well."

"Celia, why did you take the van this morning?"

"Margery asked me if I could pick up some food and kitchen supplies in Ripon. She said the cook needed them for tonight, and there was too much to fit in a passenger car."

"Why didn't she ask Robert?" asked her husband?

"She said he was off on another errand," said Celia.

Richard shook his head. "That's strange. I saw him down at the end of the garden, working on the tractor. He was there most of the morning."

"I think we need to go see that van tomorrow," said Frederick.

"What good's that going to do?"

"It may answer a few lingering questions," said Frederick. "Happens I know the odd bit about motor vehicles."

"If you don't mind, let's keep all of this between us right now. I'm going to let you and Olympia off at The Moorlands, but I'm taking Celia home, and I'm staying the night. I'll miss the banquet, but I'll be back first thing in the morning. Please tell everybody we're fine, but I just need to be with my wife."

"I'll do that very thing," said Frederick.

"I'm so hungry I could eat a dead rat," said Olympia.

Frederick shuddered. "How delicate of you, my love. Would you like chips with that?"

"We missed our lunch, and they only gave us tea and cream crackers in the hospital," added Celia.

"All will be made well. Special retreat feast at The Moorlands for Frederick and Olympia, and Indian take-away out of the cartons for us. Bon appetit!"

When Frederick and Olympia came through the front door, the two were greeted by a cheering crowd. Everyone wanted to hear the details and see for themselves that their favorite American really was relatively unscathed.

"She's still a bit wobbly on her pins, but I'm sure a glass of wine would do her a power of good."

"Mind reader,"whispered a grateful Olympia.

When they were seated at dinner, Olympia relayed Richard's message. She assured all present that Celia was bruised and shaken up but, like herself, grateful to be alive to tell the tale. Olympia added that she only wished she could say the same for the van.

After the meal and the speeches, Gillian suggested they all take a wander out to the pub for a celebratory pint. This was received with cheers all around except for Olympia who was already yawning and rubbing her eyes.

"I'm prescribing a long hot bath for my wife while you all go out on the town. We've both had a long and rather, ahem, adventurous day."

Frederick, as always, was the master of the understatement.

After the mandatory bath Olympia was still too agitated to sleep, so she turned the bedside light away from Frederick's side of the room and picked up Miss Winslow's diary.

November 28, 1862

It is snowing and looks as though it will continue throughout the day and into the night. Little Jonathan still does not understand snow, although he can say the word and often tries to eat it. He still is amazed at the cold wet whiteness on his face and tongue.

With Louisa here my blessings are twofold. I have more time to write, and my dear friend Richard is free to visit whenever he fancies. The village tongues are wagging again. If they only knew!

More anon, LFW

Twenty-Four

The last day of any conference is a curious mix of sadness about leaving friends and the pleasant anticipation of going home and getting back into the regular routine. Both Richard and Celia were on site by breakfast time, and like Olympia the night before, assured one and all that Celia was bowed but not beaten, and she was glad to be in one piece and back to work. What the conferees could not know was the turmoil swirling below the surface of the smiles and the well-wishing.

Richard had planned a short morning wrap-up and next-steps meeting with Olympia in attendance. Following that, a few minutes of prayer and shared reflection, and then out the door and see you all next year … maybe.

In her office, besides being stiff all over from the impact of the crash, Celia was firmly wedged between the devil and the deep blue sea, and neither option seemed particularly appealing. She had no alternative but to tell the board what she'd learned from the accountant, but should she say anything to Margery before or after she met with the board? Courtesy and human kindness dictated the former. Of course, Margery's involvement with any irregularity was technically supposition, but only one person had access to the books and the money, and only one person had become agitated when Celia asked to see the old guest registers.

Speaking—well thinking, really—about Mrs. M., where is she? It's almost ten, Celia thought. The woman is never late, and I can't remember her ever missing a day's work. Is it possible she's learned that I've contacted the board, and if so, what then? Is she hiding somewhere? Not likely. Has she left town? Even less likely. Admittedly she didn't know the woman very well, but she did know Margery Mosely never walked away from anything she set her mind to. So where was she?

Celia was just about to go out and try and find Robert when the man himself came into her office.

"Margery wanted me to tell you she'll be in late today. She's gone off to see the doctor."

"Oh, dear, nothing serious, I hope. I don't remember her saying anything about feeling poorly."

Robert looked acutely uncomfortable. "Uh, she said something about it being a female thing. Didn't say what, though, and I'm not one to ask."

Celia said she understood and thanked him, but she still didn't have the answer to her question of when to tell Margery about the meeting. *I suppose it all depends on when she gets back,* she told herself. *I've called the meeting for two this afternoon. Certainly she'll be back by then, and if she isn't, then it will be afterward.* She shuddered involuntarily. *Surely this is going to be every bit as unpleasant as the car accident, and very likely more so.*

"Thank you, Doctor. Yes, I do understand, one or two before bedtime with water, don't operate any heavy machinery, and I'm to call if I experience any nausea. I'll be off now. I'm late for work." On the way back, Margery turned into Tesco's. Thomas was almost out of cat food, and she and Robert needed biscuits for their tea. If she wasn't too long about it, she should be back in time for lunch.

After calling the local police to find out where The Moorlands' van had been towed, Fredrick borrowed Richard's car and set off to do some investigation of his own. People were often surprised to learn that he knew his way around the inside of an automobile engine. "Poverty and desperation," he would tell them if they asked. "In my youth I had no money, so the cars I was able to afford usually didn't run. That part was up to me."

As he drove along with all the windows down, Frederick inhaled the green and pleasant beauty of his homeland. There was no green like English green anywhere in the world. Eight thousand years of drizzle and sheep droppings, he told himself, nothing like it. But when he reached the salvage yard, his countryside euphoria quickly turned to horror when he saw what was left of the van. It was a miracle anyone had survived. It was a crumpled mess.

He asked the attendant for help opening the back so he could get a look at the engine, but when he did it didn't take him long to find what he was after. Several wires and cables, leading to God knows where, had obviously been tampered with. Some were broken clear through, while others looked as if they'd been deliberately frayed and could let go any time.

Frederick called for the attendant to come and verify what he'd found. Then he reached into his pocket and took out his camera. Getting as close as he could, he snapped several pictures of what he'd found. Finally, he asked the attendant how long it would be before the van was due to be crushed, and if need be, could that be postponed until the police had a chance to inspect it?

The man said it could and cheerfully accepted the tenner Frederick held up between two fingers. His next stop was police headquarters. No point in calling in to The Moorlands yet. He was only halfway through his agenda, and besides, it was time for his elevenses. Surely there would be a café somewhere along the way, and then, after going to the police, Frederick needed to have a little chat with Robert Mosely.

Once the retreat was officially declared over, Olympia dragged herself and her computer into the internet room. Her muscle aches and spasms had been getting worse by the hour, and by eleven she wanted nothing more than to sit in a quiet space and check her e-mail and play solitaire. Sleep was out of the question. She hurt too much. Maybe she should take one of the pain killers the doctor had given her? No, that would knock her out, and she didn't want that. Two small aspirin now and a large glass of wine later on.

Her e-mail turned out to be a pleasant diversion. She had messages from all three kids, two from Father Jim, and about thirty urgent messages from Nigerian princes offering her Viagra and/or penis enhancers. The ads were pesky, but they did make her laugh as she methodically deleted them. Considering the events of the last twenty-four hours, she needed a little comic relief.

Seven days ago she'd arrived knowing she was expected to do more than help out at a religious leadership retreat. No one ever explained to her how much more, but who could possibly have seen any of this coming? Somebody had, and given that she and Frederick were leaving the next day, she wondered if she'd ever learn the full story. Olympia turned back to her computer.

Rather than trying to decide which of the real e-mails to open first, Olympia decided simply to start at the bottom and work her way up. Father Jim was first on the list. He got right to the point and suggested Celia install a program on The Moorlands' computer that would allow another person, usually a repair technician with the proper password, to get into the system and ferret out bugs and viruses. This would also allow someone with advanced skills to go through everything and, if there was a hidden file, to open it.

With that out of the way, he began a new paragraph, telling her he had some real options on the employment front and wishing she were there to discuss them with him. One was a college chaplaincy position that would involve some teaching, and the other was as a chaplain/social worker in Dorchester, not far from his old Parish of St. Bartholomew's. He ended by suggesting they Skype again and suggested a couple of times.

Randall, the younger of her two sons, wrote that he hoped she was having a good time, he was thinking about taking a couple of intensive January courses so he could finish early, his car needed a new muffler and when would she be back? She laughed out loud. Randall always could pack an entire novel into one paragraph.

Malcolm wrote only that they had something to tell her when she got back, and where would she and Frederick be in July of next year? Olympia did the math, eight months from now, ten months after the wedding. Malcolm never could keep a secret.

Laura had attached two pictures, one of Erica learning to eat with a spoon and a shot of the table set for her first dinner guest. She went on to say she was feeling much better now and starting to have something like a social life again. Finally she asked if Olympia and Frederick might see their way clear to coming out for Christmas, and there was someone she'd like them to meet.

That one Olympia responded to at once. "New boyfriend???"

The response came back instantly, "No, mother, girlfriend. Her name is Gerry."

Olympia was instantly sorry she'd asked. Laura was understandably wary of relationships after the fiasco with Erica's father. She wrote back, "Let me see what we can do. I'm giving it a definite maybe right now and leaning toward yes. I need to talk to Frederick. Luv-u!"

Jim's second e-mail, gave more details of the computer sharing program and asked for those further developments she might be able to share. In a postscript he added he'd discovered a new wine he was anxious to try out on them, and when exactly would they be coming home?

How the hell do I answer that one? she asked herself and then typed two words, "Stay tuned."

~

When Margery left Tesco's, she drove directly to the Hare and Dog and left the car behind the pub and well out of view from the street. After locking the doors she went back using a footpath rather than the main road. When she got back to her cottage she methodically put away the biscuits and the cat food, collected her purse, a notebook and the passkey which gave her access to every room in the manor. After a last look around the cottage she stepped outside, crossed the staff parking area and entered the main house through the second back entrance. Thomas tried to follow her, but she shooed him away with fond words, locked the door and started up the stairs.

She was sure no one would see her because they'd all be in the dining room having a quiet post-retreat lunch, and none of the windows overlooked the car park. Celia and the others, even Robert, would be eating together, as was the custom when a group left. They would all be breathing a collective sigh of relief and reviewing the events of the past week.

It had been quite a week, but somehow she'd managed to stay on course. Celia might be calling for an executive meeting of the board, but Margery was way ahead of her. Nothing could stop her now, not a meeting, not a chartered accountant, not even the threat of going to prison. It wouldn't happen. All those years ago she promised herself the last word, and nothing short of that would do. Margery had taken care of every last detail. That's how she did things.

Thomas waited outside by the door for a time and even tried a piteous yowl or two, but when it was clear he was having no effect, he eventually turned away and busied himself with a leaf that needed chasing.

Sitting inside with the others, Robert kept looking toward the door, expecting to see his wife. When they'd all finished eating and she still hadn't returned, he asked Celia if she might check the answerphone in the office and see if maybe there was a message. When that produced nothing, Robert began to be concerned. It was not like her to do anything without telling him or someone else. Margery was a woman who needed everything in its place, herself included. So where was she?

He started back to his cottage and then remembered she'd gone to see the doctor that morning. Possibly, he reasoned, it had taken longer than expected, and she didn't think to call. Or maybe the doctor had ordered some tests, and that's where she was.

Robert heard something behind him and turned to see Thomas trotting toward him with a dead leaf in his mouth. He leaned down and gave the animal a thorough ear scratching.

"Have y'brought me a prezzie, Thomas? Come on then, boy, I suppose you expect a treat for it."

Robert and a high-tailed Thomas went into the cottage, and Robert pulled the door shut behind them.

Twenty-Five

The meeting of The Moorlands' Board of Governors was called for two in the afternoon. Celia asked Annette Darcie if she might have some tea and cakes and pitchers of water available in the conference room. In the moments before people began to arrive, Celia directed the set-up from a seat by the fire with her crutches leaning on the wall beside her. She, like Olympia, was in serious pain from the accident the day before, but, she reminded herself, she'd rather be upright and in pain at The Moorlands than dead on a slab in a cold dark room. Then she realized that despite the tensions and the crises of the week, she was not having any abdominal pain or associated inconveniences.

Maybe there was something to Olympia's warning after all. She thought about the biscuit she didn't eat and remembered it was still wrapped it its little napkin somewhere in her handbag. Something else to follow up on, but not right now. She looked up and gave a little wave as the board members began coming into the room and felt the ambient temperature begin to drop. Not a one of them was smiling.

Later, when it was almost all over but the shouting (and the wailing and the gnashing of teeth), Celia told them they needed to come to a consensus about how they wanted to proceed. She said she'd seen the boxes containing the account books on Wednesday, but they'd since vanished. Mrs. Mosely was not there at present, but when she did come back, what did they suggest as a course of action with regard to her? Lastly, who or how many of them would go with her to the office of Daniel Kaiser, ACA, on Monday and see it all in real time?

Finally it was decided that when Margery returned, Celia would say nothing other than a problem had been discovered in the accounting system. She was to tell Margery the computer had been locked, and she was not to do any kind of work until it could all be sorted. If she insisted on knowing why this was so, she was to call Michael Herlihy, the chairman, who would explain the situation.

To Robert she was to say only that there appeared to be an irregularity in the accounting, and the board was working on it.

After the board members left Celia pulled herself to her feet, positioned her crutches and hobbled out of the room. She looked into the adjoining office, but it was dark; Margery had still not come back. Celia knew the woman had a couple of allies on the board and wondered if perhaps she'd been alerted and taken flight. Then what? Celia had no answer. At the moment she could barely put one foot in front of the other. She was in pain, she was emotionally and physically exhausted, and she needed to find a place to lie down before she fell down.

Olympia powered down her computer and went in search of Frederick, only to learn that he hadn't yet returned. Like Celia, she ached all over and was considering another long hot bath when Thomas the cat scampered by with Robert Mosely in hot pursuit.

"Come here, y'daft puss," he huffed, lunging for the cat and scooping him up. "Sorry about that, he's looking for Margery. He gets all over himself when one of us isn't about. To be honest with you, so am I. It's not like her to be away for so long without calling in. Dead nuts on routine, she is."

Olympia nodded and winced from the pain in her neck and shoulders. It was an effort even to speak. "From what little I know about your wife, I certainly have to agree with you."

"Reverend Brown, about yesterday."

"Oh, do please call me Olympia, and what about yesterday? It was scary, and I'm in pain, but at least it means I'm alive."

Robert lifted the squirming cat up onto his shoulder and scuffled his feet. "I have to tell you, I feel horrible about what happened. I feel like it was my fault, but I checked that thing from top to bottom only the day before. It's old, I'll tell you, but it's sound. In fact, your Frederick was out there with me."

Olympia held up her hand to stop him and immediately wished she hadn't. It hurt like hell.

"Robert, it was an accident. All that's lost is the van. Celia and I are a little shaken up, but we will both be fine. You didn't do anything wrong. The only thing I don't understand is, one minute the brakes worked, and the next minute they didn't."

"That may have been what saved your life."

"What do you mean?"

"If you had stopped, the lorry would likely have smashed into you. As it was, you made it across the street."

"It was a lovely old van," said Olympia with a wistful smile.

"Aye," said Robert, turning away. "Come on, Thomas, let's go back and wait for your mother."

When he left, Olympia remained standing in the foyer. He's a good man, she thought. I wish I could say the same for his wife, but the two are really chalk and cheese. You wonder what attracts people and keeps them together. It was an age old question, and Olympia was in desperate need of her bath and some more aspirin. Then it occurred to her that Frederick still wasn't back from his investigations. That could prove interesting, as well. Olympia turned toward the stairway; it looked like Mount Everest from where she stood. However, there was a bathtub and plenty of hot water up there, and she was in serious pain.

Frederick came back mid-afternoon to find his wife squeaky clean and fast asleep. Good, he thought, looking down at her, she needs it. Next on his list was to find Richard and Celia and let them know what he'd found.

As he went down the stairs he couldn't help but notice how quiet it was without the retreat people. I suppose there's a rhythm to all of this, he thought, busy, then quiet, busy, then quiet. The quiet was almost unnerving—too quiet, he thought, and then wondered why that was and why it bothered him.

Upstairs in her room Olympia was startled awake by the clanging of the clock next to her bed. When she got her bearings and realized what it was, she also knew Leanna was telling her that somewhere, something was terribly wrong.

"I wish you could talk and tell me what it is," she said to the clock.

The clock said nothing.

Option two was to look in Miss Winslow's diary. Sometimes when the clock went off like this, she would find something that gave her a clue in reading the woman's actual words.

"Ping," said the clock.

Olympia nodded, winced and pulled open the drawer of the nightstand where she kept the diary.

December 3, 1862

Snow again today, but I have wood in the bin and food in the larder and the most whimsical and practical of secrets. Who knew it would be Aunt Louisa who would solve the "Richard dilemma" to everyone's satisfaction and delight?

In our many chats by the fire, Richard and I have shared our most secret of secrets, and in so doing admitted to our deep caring for one another. So why do we not marry? I have confessed in these pages, I have no intention to marry, because I will lose my home and property. Richard has no desire to marry ... because he doesn't fancy women. Louisa and I have known this for some time, and it does not affect our friendship in any way. Why should it? But people talk, and people can be cruel.

It might have been the sherry the other evening. Louisa did have two glasses, and her spectacles were sitting a bit sideways on the end her nose, but she has made a suggestion that may be the solution to what has become a rather awkward social situation.

At Christmas time Richard and I will declare to all and sundry that we have gone off and been quietly married. If anyone asks (and no doubt someone will), we will say we plan to keep both houses because we are too set in our ways to move. We will, of course, not be legally married, but who will be the wiser? This way we can spend as much time together as we wish, and Jonathan will have a man in his life that he adores. For the first time in a long time, I am truly excited at the prospect of the coming holidays, and my darling mischievous Aunt Louisa has decided to make us a wedding cake for Christmas dinner.

More anon, LFW

Twenty-Six

Frederick and Richard were off in a corner of the downstairs sitting room.

"Bloody hell," said Richard when he'd heard the full extent of Frederick's investigation of the remains of the van. "The only person here who would know how to do something like that would be Robert Mosely, and in my wildest dreams I can't imagine him ever doing it. It's just not in him."

"I agree, but then who?" said Frederick.

"Let's go and get Celia and Olympia."

"Olympia's sleeping."

"No, I'm not."

"What did you want to talk to us about?" Celia was leaning heavily on her crutches. "Olympia's just come and called me in."

"Everything! Come in and sit down, and I'll go find Annette and ask her to bring us some tea." Richard sidestepped the two women and left the room.

"I could use a glass of wine," moaned Olympia.

"After the tea, m'love," said Frederick. "We all need clear heads."

When Richard returned, Frederick had made the two women as comfortable as he could. He'd propped them with pillows and lifted their feet and even opened a window a crack for some cool, fresh air. They were going to need it. Richard asked Frederick to tell the two women what he'd found.

"So it was deliberate. Somebody wanted that van to crash," said Olympia when he'd finished.

"If it is true, and someone really did cut and fray those cables, then we are not only dealing with embezzlement but attempted murder, as well," said Frederick.

Celia shook her head. "I'm not sure whoever did it wanted to hurt Olympia. I can be pretty sure I was the target."

"And I'm collateral damage," said Olympia.

"This is not funny," said Frederick.

"Sorry, darling, it's an old habit. I crack jokes when I'm scared witless."

"Olympia!"

She was saved further scolding by the welcome arrival of Annette and the tea cart. "Shall I pour the tea?" she asked.

"No, thank you, Annette, we can manage."

She stood for a moment, looking at the people sitting in front of her. "There's something amiss, isn't there, Mrs. Attison?"

Celia hesitated before responding. "Yes, Annette, there is, but I'd prefer that you said nothing to anyone out there for the moment. I'll be calling a general meeting of all the staff either by the end of today or at the very latest tomorrow morning, when I'll explain everything. But for now may I ask you to keep even this much in confidence?"

Annette lowered her eyes. "Of course, Mrs. Attison, and I do thank you for telling me."

"And Annette, do please close the door firmly as you go out."

When they were alone it was Richard who poured their tea and began the conversation.

"Do you think you did the right thing by telling her, Celia?"

"Strange as it may appear to all of you, yes. She will either do as asked and keep our confidence, or she won't, but don't think for a minute she's the only one who knows something's in the wind. Of all of them, she and Robert Mosely are the only two who will speak the truth to your face as well as behind your back. I trust her."

"Speaking of Robert Mosely, I'm beginning to worry about the whereabouts of Margery. It's completely out of character for her to disappear without a word." Celia held out her hand for the teacup Richard was offering.

"I bumped into him earlier today. He was trying not to let it show, but he's concerned, as well. Funny, even the cat seems agitated."

Olympia thought about her own two cats. "They do that, you know. Animals will pick up on their owners' moods, and speaking of moods, Frederick, our own dear Miss Winslow has added her two cents' worth."

"How so?"

"What are you two talking about?" asked Richard.

"It's a long story, too long for now, but I promise to tell you when we are not so taken up with more serious issues. Sufficient for now is to say it's a husband and wife thing."

Celia would have laughed, except it would have hurt too much. "We have our own code words. They come in handy. Now where were we?"

Olympia responded. "Let me outline it as I understand it. Might be good since I'm technically an observer—and I suppose a victim as of yesterday. That was a rather unpleasant surprise, I must say."

"Go ahead, Olympia," said Richard.

"When we got here I could feel a real tension among the staff, *sotto voce* mutterings, dark looks and the like. Margery Mosely took no pains to hide her dislike of Celia and all but called her useless in front of us."

Celia groaned and shook her head.

"That first night we came in here and sat around with a group of ramblers. They said they'd been coming here for years and then told us all about the general decay and the financial issues here. They said they didn't expect the place to stay open much longer."

Celia picked up the story. "Then we came, and I pulled you both aside and told you my troubles and my suspicions. I knew something was terribly out of order, and I was planning to meet with the board, but someone unbeknownst to me went and cancelled the meeting."

"But you got violently ill and had to leave," said Frederick.

"Yes, and right now the rest of me may be in rough shape, but my stomach and lower intestine are just fine, thank you very much. I've had no problems at all, I think because I did as you suggested, Olympia. I have not eaten anything here that I didn't bring in or prepare myself."

"Then I go off to the pub and learn about Margery's secret history with this place."

"Bloody hell, I'd almost forgotten about that in all the kerfuffle after the accident," said Richard.

"I haven't," said Olympia.

She was shifting about and trying to find a more comfortable position, but there wasn't one, so she continued. "Why didn't she tell anyone about her past? One wonders if her husband even knew."

"That's a lot of anger and outrage building up over an entire lifetime," said Frederick.

Richard nodded in agreement. "And by the look of it, several hundreds of thousands of pounds, as well, most likely lifted slowly, drop by drop, out of here. She was the only one who had access to everything."

"How could this go on for so long and not be noticed? Didn't anyone ever think to question her? Most organizations have regular audits. Why not this place?" asked Olympia.

"We did have regular financial reports. Margery did them regular as clockwork. She'd bring us the facts and figures all nicely lined up on bright, shiny paper. I understand that once, years ago, someone asked her for a clarification on something, and the woman almost went into cardiac arrest. I heard she went on about how she'd always been trusted, never questioned, and if people wanted a new bookkeeper … well, you can imagine the response." Celia laid her head back on the pillow behind her. She was exhausted.

"I see," said Olympia.

"So one day when she was out I went into her office and downloaded the whole accounting file onto a flash drive and brought it over to Mr. Kaiser. As I said, there was only five years' worth of data, but it was enough that he found a false vendor. That's when he called me."

"And somehow Margery got wind of it?"

"I'm not sure how and probably not the full extent of it. Maybe it was when I asked for the attendance figures. She did not want me going up into the attic. I know why now. The accounts boxes were up there. I saw them, and then I heard the fire alarm and realized I was locked in up there." She shook her head. "I've had quite a week, haven't I?"

"Not half. I think it's time we called the police," said Richard.

Celia nodded. "I agree. You do it, will you, darling?"

"Hang on a minute, what about us? Do we stay on and help, or do we go? I have photographic evidence, and my wife was driving the car that crashed, and we are due at my sister's house by Sunday at the latest."

"And where the hell is Margery Mosely?" said Richard Attison.

"Let's sort Olympia and me out first. We can stay at least until Sunday morning. That gives us time to make formal statements and hand over the photographs. We plan to be in the UK for another week and could extend if necessary."

"Thank you, Frederick. Let me call the police and see what they say. They are going to just love me for springing this on them right before the weekend."

"Tough," snapped Celia.

"What about the staff?"

"Call the police, Richard. Once that's done, I'll call in the staff and tell them we have a serious problem which unfortunately is going to involve a police investigation and ask them all please to cooperate. "

"If they can find that money, will The Moorlands be able to continue?" asked Olympia.

"From what Daniel Kaiser indicated, it surely will and then some."

"Is that what you'd like to see, Celia?"

She shook her head. "At this moment I honestly don't know. I just have to get through the staff meeting, and that is going to take my very last ounce of energy. Tell the police they can come tomorrow. I'm not going to be any good tonight."

They were interrupted by a knock at the door.

"Come in, "called Richard.

It was Robert Mosely. He was ashen faced.

"Good heavens, man, has something happened to Margery?"

He shook his head. "I don't know. They found the car parked behind the pub. It's locked, and the keys are missing."

"Uh oh," whispered Frederick as Richard got up and hastened to help the man to a seat.

"Do you think …?"

He shook his head miserably. "I don't know what to think. She's not been herself these last few days. I suppose that's why she went to see the doctor."

"Call the police, Richard."

Twenty-Seven

Once the police had been called, Olympia and Frederick stayed in the sitting room with Robert while Celia and Richard went out to speak to the staff. She planned to tell them as little as she could and still be truthful. She would tell them pretty much what she'd told Annette, that she'd recently become aware of a significant financial issue which had the potential to affect all of them. As soon as she had more information herself she would share it with them at once, but in the meantime their jobs were secure for now, and they were to carry on as best they could.

She wondered if she should say anything about Margery being missing. I must be joking, she thought. Of course they know. Robert surely has told them by now. Celia limped into the dining room and took a seat at the biggest table to wait while Richard went off to round up the staff.

In the sitting room Olympia and Frederick were trying to make reassuring conversation with Robert when Thomas nosed his way through the door and into their midst.

"Daft animal, he's looking for her same as me," said Robert. Then he covered his face with his hands and began to weep.

Both Olympia and Frederick were at a loss as to what to say. How much did he know about the missing money? How much did he know about his wife's ancestral connection to The Moorlands? It was clear he'd had nothing to do with the car malfunction, but who did, and where the hell was Margery? Olympia was grateful that Thomas had elected to join them. He eased the tension and gave them something neutral to talk about while they waited for Celia and Richard to come back … and the police to arrive.

Locked in one of the little used rooms upstairs, Margery was making things ready. She had only one chance, and she knew she had to get it right. But Margery didn't make mistakes, and she wouldn't now. She just needed a little more time. That would be the only thing that might be an issue, but really, who would think to look for her here? The stupid fools assumed she'd gone away. Not a bit of it. Margery Mosley had come back to the home that was rightfully hers.

When the police officers arrived, Frederick took Robert off for a cup of tea in the dining room while Richard, Celia and Olympia told the police what they knew and asked what they should do next. They explained how they were dealing with two issues, really, a possible embezzlement case and a potentially missing individual who was very likely going to be a person of interest in all of this. The older of the two officers told them that if they wanted to press charges, they would have to bring as much documentation as they could to substantiate their claim. If the authorities considered the evidence to be sufficient, they would swear out a warrant for the arrest of Margery Mosley.

Celia was twisting her fingers. "This is going to destroy Robert. When are we supposed to do this? Can't we just keep her here with us if she promises to show up at the hearing?"

The police officer looked doubtful. "I think we have to wait until we formally press charges to make that decision, and remember something else. We don't know where she is right now. If all that money is hidden away somewhere, and she is the person who put it there, she might just be on her way to Switzerland or the Cayman Islands to reclaim it. The sooner you make a formal statement, the better. It means we can get started on our end."

"I simply cannot believe this is happening," said Celia.

"Past tense, Mrs. Attison, it has happened. Now comes the sorting out bit, and that's going to take some investigation. Meanwhile, I'd like to talk to Mr. Mosley and find out what I can about his wife. We don't usually file a missing person report until they've been gone for at least forty-eight hours, but given the circumstances, I think we are justified in doing it sooner. It's the bit about the car being abandoned—that's the part I don't like."

"I don't like any of it. I do think we should ask Frederick to stay with Robert. The two seem to have struck up a bit of a friendship."

"Right, then, where do you think they are?"

"Frederick took him off for a cup of tea, so they're probably in the dining room, and if not, then they've gone back to the Mosleys' cottage."

When they left Celia turned to Olympia. "I could sleep for England right now, but I don't think I'm going to get the chance."

"Not so fast. Now we've finally got the police involved, much of this is off your shoulders. Do you see what I'm getting at? Now it's their concern."

Celia nodded. She was exhausted by it all, and the strain was evident.

"Please don't think me completely crass for saying this, Celia, but I'm famished. You said you could sleep for England. Well, I could eat for England or the US or anyone who is kind enough to feed me. I don't suppose the cook will have made anything for the staff tonight, do you?"

"That's why God gave us take-away, Olympia. When the boys in blue get off the premises, we're getting in a massive pile of fish and chips."

Later, when all that was left of their supper was a pile of greasy papers and crumpled containers, Frederick raised the subject of their leaving to Richard and Celia.

"We can stay on through Sunday morning, if you think we'll be needed, but my preference would be to get started tomorrow afternoon. I think Olympia and I could both use a transition day before we take on the wonders of my family."

Celia and Richard both looked genuinely distressed. "Olympia, I feel I owe you an apology. If I could have possibly known how this week would turn out, I never would have asked you to come on board. It's bad enough we've exhausted you, but we damn near got you killed in the process," said Richard.

Olympia held up her hand to stop him from saying any more. "I came here of my own free will, Richard. It did turn out to be a bit more than any of us bargained for, but we survived, and we may have gotten to the cause of the problem. Look at it this way: we're still here, Celia's not having stomach pains, and if we get really lucky, we might be able to retrieve some of that money."

"All this and one hell of a story to tell our grandchildren," said Frederick.

"We only have one so far, dear, but I think my son Malcolm might be increasing that number."

"Really?"

"He hinted at it in his last e-mail, along with my other son, who hinted that he might be getting married sometime next year."

"'Tis the season," said Richard.

"Speaking of that, Laura has invited us out there for Christmas. She's says she's got a friend she wants us to meet."

"Really, so she's finally started seeing someone?"

"Not in the way you think, Frederick. It's a girlfriend, but at least she's starting to make friends and get out a little bit. I was beginning to worry about her."

"So what's the plan? We stay the night and decide tomorrow? Oh, my God, Celia, you don't have another group coming in here on Sunday do you?"

Celia shook her head. "Thank heaven for small mercies, nothing until next weekend. And yes, if you two could hold off until tomorrow to decide when you are leaving, it would make me feel better. I have to tell you, I don't like the idea that Margery's gone missing. It's quite unsettling."

Olympia nodded and covered a huge yawn. "I have to go to bed, or I'm going to expire right here in front of everyone."

"Allow me, Madame." Frederick stood and held out his arm.

"I believe we'll stay the night here ourselves," said Celia. "I know of a couple of rooms that don't get much use and should be made up. Thank you, both of you. I don't think I would have survived this without you."

Olympia stood with some difficulty and turned to Celia. "If I didn't think it would kill both of us, I'd lean over and hug you, but I think we've each had enough pain for one day."

Celia blew them a kiss. "Amen and goodnight, my friends. Sleep well. Believe it or not, I think I will, as well."

Twenty-Eight

The next morning Frederick went downstairs with the intention of getting them both a cup of tea and learning if Margery Mosely had turned up. She had not. He considered going across the back parking area to see Robert, but he thought better of it. He would do it later after his tea. But then he heard, rather than saw, something in the doorway and turned to see what it was. It was Thomas, and if a cat could look miserable, it was Thomas.

Frederick changed his mind again. He would go and check on Robert. He whistled for Thomas to follow him, but the cat went in the opposite direction, looking for his mistress. Frederick found it terribly sad and wished he could comfort the poor animal. He followed the cat halfway up the stairs, picked him up and tucked him under his arm.

"Come on, old boy, you and I are going off to see yer dad."

Thomas yowled.

Upstairs in her room Olympia remained in bed, floating in and out of sleep long enough to realize that Frederick had gotten sidetracked and would not be bringing her tea. He did that. She looked at the clock that worked and decided it was time to take matters into her own hands and find some coffee. When she did so, she was pleased to note that her muscle pain had abated considerably, and simple arm and leg movements no longer caused her to wince and groan. Things were looking up. She dressed carefully and headed for the stairs.

The place was deathly quiet and eerie with it. The Moorlands was like two different places, humming and purring with life and energy when a group was in residence, and ghostly quiet and claustrophobic when it was empty as it was now. Olympia shivered. She was more than ready to get out of there. She'd had enough, and there wasn't anything more she or Frederick could do to help. The rest was up to Celia and the board and, God help them, the police.

As she was dressing she heard the sound of a toilet flushing and was surprised to find herself oddly comforted by the sound of another human being doing something very normal somewhere in that great dark pile of stones.

Downstairs, Celia and the staff, minus Robert Moseley, were gathered in the dining room, trying to make conversation and, failing that, trying to comfort one another—and failing that, as well. The collective sadness and fear hung in the air like a cold grey mist. Celia desperately wanted to be able to reassure them, but at the moment it was simply not possible. She called for their attention.

"I want you all to know I'm working with the board and the police, and we are doing everything we can to find some definitive answers for us all. Not knowing is the worst, and if it's any comfort to you whatsoever, I don't know either, but I am doing everything I can to get it sorted. I do know there's enough money to pay you all through to the end of the year. After that I'm afraid I can't make any promises. I do understand if some of you want to move on as quickly as possible, but I hope you'll bear with us for as long as you can.

"I'm going to meet with the accountant and the police on Monday. We don't have anyone coming in here until next weekend, and by then we'll know something. I can't exactly say that until then, it's business as usual, but I can say we are British, and somehow we will muddle through it all together."

She looked around at them all before continuing. "I refuse to give up hope, and I need you all to chivvy me along when I feel overwhelmed by it all. You have my word that I will not give up until the authorities close the place down and lock me out of my office. Barring that, I'm here for the long haul."

There was a long silence when Celia finished speaking, and then, one by one, the people in the room began to stand and declare their support. She couldn't believe her eyes, and her ears. Even Mrs. Loring stuck her red face out of the kitchen door and shouted, "I'm 'ere, and I'm stayin' ere." It was the first time since Celia had taken the job that she felt their united support and approval. Tears welled up in her eyes, and she dropped back into her chair but not before whispering, "Thank you everyone, I'll certainly do my best."

In the caretaker's cottage Frederick and Robert were doing the best they could to sidestep the obvious and somehow continue to make companionable noises to one another. They were on their second cup of tea, and it was rapidly cooling when Frederick decided to take a chance.

"Robert, it's not my place to pry, but better me than the police. Is there anything you can think of that might cause your wife to leave without a word to anyone?"

Robert picked at the sleeve of his jumper and said nothing. It was clear he was thinking about how to respond. Finally he spoke.

"Do you remember me telling you that you can't assume you know someone, even if you've been married to them for over thirty years?"

Frederick nodded.

"Margery's always been the brainy one. She's the reader, and she's the one who keeps the accounts, our own and those over there." He gestured with a tilt of his head toward the manor house.

"I'm not complaining, mind you, but she's never been what you'd call cheerful. I suppose over time I've just gotten used to it. Maybe if we'd had children she might have been different, but it never happened."

Frederick tried a different tack. "Has anything happened recently that might have affected her? Has someone said something to her, criticized her in some way?"

Robert looked even more troubled now. He took a deep breath. "A few months ago she told me something about herself I never knew. I think it explains a good bit of why she is the way she is."

"The police are going to be asking questions, lots more questions about why she might have run off like this. Do you think what she told you might have anything to do with her leaving?"

Robert nodded but said nothing.

"I'm not asking that you tell me what it was, but is it something you are willing to tell the police?"

Robert bit his lip and shook his head.

Frederick swallowed the last of his cold tea and made a really ugly face. This caused Robert to chuckle and eased the morbid tension in the room.

"I need to be getting back; shall I let the cat out?"

Thomas had been sitting and staring at the door for the whole time they'd been talking.

"Y'might as well. Poor daft little sod will just sit there and moan if you don't. He's looking for her, you know. They don't understand, do they?"

"You'd be surprised at what they understand and what they don't. I think animals can read our minds."

"Thank you for coming to see me, Frederick. You will let me know if you hear anything, won't you?"

"Of course, Robert, and the same goes for you. If she calls in, do let Celia know at once. We're all concerned."

"Aye," said Robert.

Frederick set his tea cup in the sink and followed the cat out the door.

Frederick found Olympia back upstairs in their room, standing in front of an open suitcase and two piles of clothes.

"Laundry on this side and still wearable on this." She indicated which was which.

"So what do you think, pack up and leave right after lunch, or leave as soon as we can and stop at a friendly pub along the way?"

Olympia thought for a moment. "Let's see what Richard and Celia would prefer. I feel as if we're leaving them with an unexploded bomb in their hands."

"Yes, love, but it's their bomb. We can't do any more than we already have to defuse it except wish them well. Right?"

"Good idea, as usual. Let's offer to stay on for lunch. It will give us ample time to sort and pack. If they'd prefer to get on with things themselves, they'll tell us, will they not?"

"Likely not. They're English, which means they'll be polite."

"We're not stupid, darling. We can read between the lines as well as the next person."

"Point made, but since I, too, am English, why don't I go down and see which way the wind is blowing? I can probably read between English lines better than you can."

After he left Olympia continued sorting and packing. If they waited until after lunch, she could get some laundry done. That would make things easier on the next leg of the journey. What kind of an impression would she make on her new in-laws if the first words out of her mouth were, "Hi, I'm Olympia, I've just married your brother, so can you please take me to your washing machine?" No, that wouldn't do.

She looked around for something she might put the laundry into and heard, or thought she heard, the sound of something hitting the floor above her head. She stopped and looked toward the ceiling.

"Miss Winslow—Leanna, have you gone off for a walk? Did you trip or drop something up there?"

Not that Olympia expected an answer, but more and more of late, she realized, she actually was getting a response from her beloved Miss Winslow. Usually it was the clock sounding off by itself or in response to a direct question. But sometimes it came through the diary, and other times, although she could not be sure, it would be a word or a book title or even a Bible verse that would come into her consciousness.

Over the years since she'd realized what was behind these moments of curious clarity, she'd learned to pay attention. Meanwhile, the clock on the night stand remained silent.

"Hmmm."

"Humming or thinking, darling? I never know which." Frederick was back. "They'd like us to stay on for lunch, sort of a post mortem, I suppose."

"God, Frederick, can't you think of any other way to put it? Given the circumstances, that's positively morbid."

"Sorry, love. They've invited Robert, as well."

Olympia grimaced. "That's not going to be easy. Still no word about Margery?"

"Nothing, I'm afraid."

"I'm afraid, too, Frederick. I'm trying not to think the worst."

"I think we all are, but for heaven's sake don't say that to Robert."

"I wouldn't think of it."

Twenty-Nine

Celia asked to have lunch served in the sitting room where they could be more private. She said she wanted some time with them so she could thank them for all they had done and tried to do, and it was time to be honest with Robert.

As they descended the stairs Olympia remarked to Frederick on the ghostly quiet of the place when there were no guests to breathe life and energy into the rooms and the corridors.

"I'll be glad to be on our way, Olympia, and to cheer us both up, I planned a little side trip surprise for us."

Olympia didn't know whether to be pleased or worried, but she agreed she needed some fresh air and a complete change of scenery before she did anything else at all. On the other hand, there was Frederick's sense of direction to consider. Maybe that was the surprise. If it meant putting The Moorlands' dark corridors and dusty stairwells behind them, she was all for it.

"Come and sit over here, and do please pull the door shut behind you." Celia waved them in. Olympia still wasn't used to the custom of shutting herself in and out of every room she entered or exited but was quickly assured it was a leftover from pre-central heating days of yore. She didn't argue the point.

"Robert not here yet?" asked Frederick.

"He's on his way, poor bugger. By the look of him he didn't sleep a wink last night. We called the police this morning, first thing, but they hadn't come up with anything new as of then."

Olympia was still shaking her head in despair when Robert shuffled into the room. No one spoke, because there was nothing to say, at least until they were all seated together.

Celia invited them to help themselves to food and drink, and when he shook his head, she begged Robert at least to have some bread and butter and a cup of tea.

"Robert, none of us knows what to do or say about Margery, but whatever it is or will be, you are going to need some food in your stomach."

"Oh, all right then, bread and butter and a cup of tea."

Olympia prepared it for him, and Celia began to speak.

"I've set an appointment with the accountant and the board of governors for Monday morning. When they are fully appraised of the situation, then we will meet alone and decide what to do next." She turned to Robert. "I'm sorry you have to hear this, Robert, but it's best you hear it here alone with us and away from the others. The board will have to decide how to proceed, whether to press charges or to wait and see if there is a way to salvage The Moorlands."

"Why would you not press charges?" asked Frederick.

"We can't press charges, we can only begin a formal investigation. The person of interest is not among us, and we have no idea where she might be."

"If it's me you are talking about, then I'm right here. What is it you want to know? I'm prepared to tell you everything."

Five people turned and gasped in unison. Robert dropped his teacup and began to weep. Margery Moseley was standing in the open doorway with Thomas at her feet.

"I have no right to ask this of you, but considering the circumstances, might I join you?"

After the initial pandemonium subsided, Margery carefully closed the door behind her and joined the others gathered around the fire. Celia held up a cup of tea, which Margery accepted at once.

"I wouldn't mind a bit of that bread and cheese, as well. I haven't eaten in twenty-four hours." She pulled up a chair, and the minute she was in it, Thomas was in her lap, pawing on her knees and purring his furry little heart out.

Olympia got out of her chair and prepared a small plate of buttered bread, slices of cheese and some grapes. Thus seated with cat on lap and food in hand, Margery began to tell the story.

Most of them knew the background details. Frederick had learned it all from the barman at the pub and shared it with the others. Margery herself had told her husband some months ago on that warm afternoon in the garden. None of them could have been prepared for the rest of the story.

"When I learned that my grandmother died in pain and shame, and my mother suffered the mark of that disgrace all of her life, I vowed I would find a way to make it right. One day I would take back what was rightfully hers ... and mine. Getting the job here seemed almost like an act of God, saying this was my due and even pointing the way.

"I began in penny numbers just to see if I could get away with it. No one noticed, and over the years the numbers got larger. Then, when I realized the potential of what I was doing, I actually went to the library and read up on embezzlement, old newspapers and such, and learned how to do it right. I invented a false vendor and started moving much greater sums of money."

"Margery ..." Robert started forward.

Celia held up her hand. "Let her finish. I know this is terrible for both of you, but this is what she wants to do, and I believe we should allow her to do it."

He nodded. His face was a mask of sadness and tragic understanding.

"It was going along according to plan until they hired Celia; then it all started to go off. By then I had everything on the computer, and it was much easier to move things around, but you had a sharp eye. I tried to make you resign by making you look stupid and incompetent. I even asked the staff to help me by telling them I was trying to save all our jobs." She shook her head.

"I did a good job, and they actually believed I had your best interests at heart. I told them this was not the place for you, which you simply didn't understand, and it was up to us to make it happen."

"Crikey," whispered Richard.

Celia spoke slowly. "Was it you who was making me sick?"

Margery nodded. "You can find anything you want on the computer. Phenolthaline is the primary ingredient in most laxatives. It's a white powder, and it's odorless and tasteless. I put it in the icing on the biscuits we gave you. Not a lot. I didn't want to kill you, just enough to keep you feeling poorly."

Celia remembered the biscuit that was still in her handbag. "Could that stuff actually kill someone if they took enough of it?" she asked.

Margery nodded and continued. "It all came to a head when I learned you'd gone to the accountant. If I didn't act at once, it would all be over."

"So you tried to kill me," said Celia.

"No, I really wanted to inconvenience you so I'd have more time. I didn't know which cable and wire in there went to what, so I frayed several of them and reckoned one would let go when you were going to get the groceries."

"And I was driving when it did," said Olympia none too gently.

Margery hung her head. "I am truly sorry I did all these things. When I learned that I hadn't killed you, you may not believe this, but I was profoundly grateful. So I chose death for myself. It meant I wouldn't spend the rest of my life in prison, but then I realized my Robert might be sent to prison anyway as an accomplice. He doesn't deserve that. I'm the villain here, no one else. So at the last minute, I changed my mind and didn't do it."

"Didn't do what?" asked Olympia.

"Take my own life."

"Margery, love …" Robert started toward her, but she shook her head and waved him away.

"None of you are going to believe this. Something happened which I can't explain. I had done everything. I looked up how to do it. I had the tablets and everything else I needed right there. I'd written out a confession. It's still upstairs. It has the numbers and locations of the offshore bank accounts where I sent the money, all that I've just told you, and an apology to my husband."

"What happened? Why didn't you do it?"

"I said you're not going to believe this. Two things happened. Thomas found me. He found his way up to the attic and was making a terrible din outside the door. He went round to the back staircase. I was locked in one of the old servant bedrooms. Who knows, it might even have been the place where my mother was conceived."

"What was the other thing?" asked Olympia.

"That's the one I can't explain. As I said, I had everything written out. I closed the notebook and set it on the floor beside the bed. I was going to put my glasses and the car keys on top of it and then take the tablets. I deliberately didn't eat anything; the tablets would work faster on an empty stomach."

Robert was weeping again.

"When everything was in place, I tried to reach for the bottle, and something stopped my hand. I tried a second time, and it happened a second time. There was no one there, but my hand simply could not get to that container. It was most curious, but it gave me time to think, and I could hear Thomas. I began thinking of Robert and how he didn't deserve any of this. And then I realized I'd accomplished what I'd set out to do."

"I don't understand," said Richard.

"It doesn't matter how I got the money. The fact is, I had the money, and I could buy The Moorlands if I wanted to."

"And then what?"

"I realized I didn't care any longer. It was like I was free of it all. I didn't want to die at The Moorlands, I wanted to go on living even it meant going to jail. Can you believe that?"

"I can, "said Celia, "and I think we need to stop for a while and think about all we've just heard before we go any further. Believe this or not, but I thank you, Margery, from the bottom of my heart."

Stunned and weary heads nodded around the circle. In their wordless silence the only sound in the room was Thomas purring until Margery said, "There's one more thing I need to tell you."

Thirty

Out on the rolling hills the sun was getting low on the horizon, and Frederick and Olympia were on the road to an undisclosed location. For the first hour of the trip neither of them spoke as they each tried to make sense of all they'd been through and witness to. Finally Olympia interrupted the thoughtful silence.

"I wonder what will happen next."

"I'm not sure. Whatever it is, it will be up to Celia and the board and the authorities to decide. Didn't Celia say she'd be meeting with all or most of them on Monday?"

"She did, but in the space of an hour the whole picture changed. I didn't want to say it, but I really thought Margery was dead."

I don't think you were alone in that, my dear, but who could have expected such a turn of events and that part about something stopping her hand …"

"Or someone," said Olympia.

"What's that supposed to mean?"

"I wouldn't be surprised if our own dear Miss Winslow had something to do with it. I did, after all, metaphorically bring her along with us, you know—the diary and the clock."

"We'll never know, will we? And look, here we are."

Olympia squinted and read the sign. "Fountains Abbey?"

"As far as I'm concerned it's one of the loveliest places in all of England, and I think a walk through it will do us both a power of good. Are you up for a little stroll?"

Olympia thought for a moment, flexed a few leg muscles and declared she was almost fit and very much ready to go. But nothing could have prepared her for what she saw when she walked through the gate and down the hill to where the remains of a ruined abbey lay sprawled before her. Buildings, partial buildings and sometimes only the remains of foundations and jagged stone outlines where rooms had once been surrounded her and stopped her breath. So much religious architecture and history in one exquisitely beautiful and deep green place.

"Do you see why I wanted to bring you here?"

All she could do was nod. When speech finally did return, she said, "It's like being in someone else's prayer. So help me, Frederick, I swear I can feel the spirits of those men who lived here. I can see them in my mind, and here I am, standing on their sacred ground."

"This was a Cistercian monastery established in the twelfth century. Amazing, isn't it? We think we are the only ones who can build tall buildings, but those monks knew a thing or two."

"So why hasn't it been preserved? Why is it in ruins like this?"

"When King Henry the Eighth made himself the head of the English church, he dissolved the monasteries. He ordered the monks out and let people take all that lovely dressed stone and make other buildings with it. We've been reusing old buildings for centuries, perhaps even millennia. Actually, this one fared better than most, and I can't tell you why. So much is still standing here, it really gives one a sense of what it was like back then."

The light was rapidly fading. The long shafts of sunlight, which only minutes ago had shot like luminous arrows through arched openings, were suddenly gone, and in their place a cool, damp twilight was descending. The only sound was the constant wind moving through the ancient walls and windows and chittering sparrows hurrying home to their roosts and settling in for the night. Frederick wrapped his arms around his wife and kissed her neck, and then he nibbled at her ear.

Olympia didn't need a blueprint or a second invitation, but the surroundings, while romantic as hell, were not conducive to comfortable marital bliss.

"I think we need to find a place to stay the night, and the sooner the better."

"There's no one here, perhaps we could just …"

"Indeed we could, but I think we won't. I fancy a warm soft bed, not wet grass and damp stones, if you don't mind."

"But what about romance and spontaneity?"

"We can turn off the heat and leave the window open while we think of England."

Frederick laughed and released her. "Come on then, wife, you've a duty to perform."

Olympia lifted her hand, pressed it against her brow and sighed. "If I must, you know your wish is my command."

"Why don't I believe that?"

"Because you're not as stupid as you look."

On Monday morning Celia Attison, Daniel Kaiser and The Moorlands' Board of Governors were seated around a conference table in Kaiser's office. Celia had just finished laying out the details. She related the entire scope of the financial situation and, with Margery's permission, the full story of how it all came to be. After the predictable gasps of "Oh, no," and "How could this have happened?" and "Who would have suspected" subsided, she began to tell the rest of the story. She took a sip of water and cleared her throat.

"Margery takes full responsibility for what has happened. In fact, late last week she wrote everything down. You all know Margery, and as you can imagine, every detail down to the last decimal point is in order. She understands that she is guilty of the crime of embezzlement and likely some ancillary charges, and she is prepared to accept the consequences of her actions."

This produced some head nodding and murmurings of "And well she should" and "Can you imagine the cheek?" and "It's only right."

"There is, however, another way to think about all of this. Margery has access to all the money, and as you just heard, it is a considerable sum, which she is prepared to return to us in full, every last penny and the accrued interest. She deeply regrets what she did and only hopes that one day we will all find a way to forgive her."

More nodding and murmuring.

"My question to you all is, if she is truly repentant and plans to return more money than The Moorlands by itself could have ever amassed—enough to repair and update every wall and every room in the place and still have something left over to put back into the endowment—should we be the ones to cast the first stone, so to speak?"

"What exactly are you suggesting?" asked Michael Herlihy, the chairman.

"I'm suggesting a number of things to you, Michael, and to all of you. One is that we accept the money, do the necessary repairs, pay the salaries and keep The Moorlands open for business. Two is that we not press charges. Embezzlement is only a crime if the money is gone. We could think of Margery as an investment manager, only we just didn't know it."

This produced a few wry smiles and curious looks.

"My third suggestion is that we accept Margery Moseley's apology and ask her to continue as bookkeeper and financial manager."

In response to their astonished looks she added, "If we can't forgive and embrace one of our own, what kind of a Christian or any other kind of religious or ethical example are we setting for the people who come through these doors? I rest my case."

Celia dropped back into her seat and waited for the sky to fall … only it didn't.

She had indeed made her case, and if she carried it to completion, then everyone would come out a winner. The Moorlands would survive, a good financial manager would keep her job and along with it, a really good jack of all trades would continue to keep everything in the place running smoothly."

"But what about the accident?" asked Pamela Claughton, one of the younger and more forward-thinking of the governors.

"It was an accident. I was in the van when it happened, and it was terrifying, but we survived. The only loss is the van. I have chosen not to press charges."

Only Daniel Kaiser remained silent through it all. This was not what he'd expected. It wasn't what anyone could have expected or anticipated. They were all in unchartered territory, and they were slowly, one by one, negotiating the waters to safety.

Thirty-One

Olympia's mother would have said it was all over but the shouting, and she would have been right. There were a few loose ends that still needed to be tied up, but they were not hers to secure. Celia and Richard Attison and The Moorlands' Board of Governors were in charge of the final outcome, and more power to them, thought Olympia. She was securely belted in, half dozing, lulled by the hum of the engines of the 747 and basking in the afterglow of an eventful, and occasionally hair-raising, two weeks. She was on her way home with her husband close beside her, and any minute now someone in a smart uniform would be bringing her food and drink. Olympia liked food and drink—and even more so when it was served it to her.

"Well, my darling, I'd say you certainly passed muster with your new relatives."

Olympia opened one eye. "You have a lovely family, Frederick. My only wish is we didn't live so far away. On the other hand, it gives me, or should I say us, reason to come here more often."

"I'm glad you feel that way. I like living in the States, but it's really good to come back to visit. I don't think I'd like to live there full-time anymore."

Olympia could hear the clinking of the beverage cart. A glass of wine would complete the picture, she thought, and when the flight attendant handed her two, she didn't give the second one back. She was glad Jim couldn't see her now. Wine that came in little bottles was truly beneath him. Not me, she thought, twisting off the top and filling her glass. I'm a philistine and proud of it.

Frederick asked for red wine, and she had a pretty standard Pinot Grigio. They held up their plastic glasses.

"To us," said Frederick.

"And to whatever comes next," added Olympia.

He groaned. "Olympia, haven't you had enough for one year?"

"The year's not over yet, my dear. The good news is we're going out to California to spend Christmas with Laura and the baby and meet Gerry."

"Gerry?"

"I told about the girlfriend she had to dinner, didn't I? Gerry was Laura's first dinner guest in the new apartment."

He nodded. "I remember now."

"Well, after my last conversation with Laura, it would appear there is more developing between them than a casual friendship."

"No kidding. Uh, how do you feel about that?"

Olympia shifted so she could speak directly to her husband.

"I'm as pleased as I could be. She's taken a huge independent step and moved all the way across the country. She's got a great job, and Erica's adjusting beautifully, but she's been lonely. Remember, Frederick, I didn't see this woman grow up. I'm still getting to know her, and now I've discovered one more dimension of who she is. I'll admit I didn't see it coming, but now that's it's here, more power to her. I want my daughter to be happy and safe, and I want her partner, whoever that may be, to love and respect her. It's what any parent would want."

"You, my darling, are not any parent, and your daughter, like you, is a very special person. Does she understand that as her step-dad I have to approve of this as well?" He raised his glass a second time. "To Laura ... and new beginnings."

While Olympia and Frederick were toasting each other at thirty-seven thousand feet, Celia and Richard Attison were sitting in a corner of The Hare and Dog, doing the self-same thing. Celia held up her glass. "I never thought I'd see the day, but here's to new beginnings at The Moorlands."

Richard raised his glass and touched the edge of hers. "So you're staying."

She nodded. "They hired me to turn the place around. Now maybe I've got half a chance to make it happen."

"We sure gave poor Olympia and Frederick a run for their money. They'll never dare to visit us again unless they come with bodyguards."

She laughed and shook her head. "I doubt that. Somehow I think Olympia can handle herself just about anywhere. Has she changed much since you last knew her?"

Richard took a thoughtful sip of his wine. "People don't change, Celia. There is one thing, though; Olympia seems a lot happier. Maybe it's connecting with her daughter, maybe it's Frederick, but she's definitely more content. Speaking of people not changing, are you sure you want to continue working with Margery? She's had a lifetime of anger driving her. What's she going to be without it?"

"I can't answer that. We'll just have to wait and see, won't we?"

"How has she been now that everything is sorted but the signing of the papers?"

"I think there is a good woman in there trying to get out. She told me something today that almost broke my heart."

Richard put down his glass. "What was that?"

"Do you remember her saying there was one more thing she needed to say?"

He nodded.

"I'm sure you heard the stories about her visiting the old man, Lord Ashton-Beckett, when he couldn't get out and about any longer. Well, according to the nastier of the village wasps, there was some question as to whether she might have actually hastened his demise."

"You're joking."

"I'm not, and one day last week when I was sitting with Margery, she asked if she could have a word."

"So what about the old man?"

"She told us she just wanted to know him. Her mother and father were both dead. She had no one in the world, and he was her only blood relative. She hated him for what he'd done to her grandmother and her mother, but in a curious way I think she also loved him. He was her grandfather, and if she's telling the truth, she never let on who she was."

"Wow," said Richard.

"Wow is right."

"You don't suppose she's going to try and claim inheritance rights, do you?"

Celia shook her head. "I asked her about that. The answer is no. When she had put away enough money to buy and then destroy the place if she wanted to, she realized she no longer did. Maybe just knowing she could was enough. We'll see."

"I think Robert is still getting over it all. It's not going to be easy for him. When I saw him today, he was not himself at all."

"He's a gentle soul, Richard. This has really upset him, but he'll eventually come around."

"How do you know?"

"He's got an excellent therapist," said Celia.

"What or who are you talking about?"

"Thomas. That cat hasn't left his side since Margery came down from the attic. After he greeted her, it's been Robert morning noon and night. It's really sweet to see. Animals can be real healers, you know."

"I do know," said Richard.

Frederick didn't waste any time getting to sleep once the meal had been removed, but despite the cheap wine and a full tummy, Olympia was still very much awake. She reached under the seat in front of her and dragged out her monster of a handbag. She was digging for Miss Winslow's diary when something in the random rubble poked her. It was the corner of an envelope which Celia had handed to her as they were saying their goodbyes. She'd stuffed it down in her bag and forgotten all about it until right now. It was a card or something very like it with her full name, Reverend Doctor Olympia Brown, written in formal script across the front. She slipped her finger under the flap and eased it open.

Inside was a folded piece of paper which, when unfolded, turned out to be the recipe for Sticky Toffee Pudding. In all the confusion at the end of that rather momentous week at The Moorlands, she'd forgotten to go back to Mrs. Loring—and now, here it was.

How kind, she thought, and then spied the handwritten words at the bottom of the page.

Dear Reverend Brown,

You never did come back for this, and I thought you might like to have something to remember us by. Remember, let the sponge cool for about five minutes before you cut into it and pour on the sauce.

All the best,

Mrs. Loring.

Olympia leaned back and smiled. It would be the perfect pudding for their Christmas dinner in California.

December 30, 1862

We are approaching the end of another year. When I first began writing in these precious pages, it was the year that my father left this earthly state. I could not ever have imagined what a curious path my life would take, much less all that has come to me as part of the journey. And now I am turning yet another page. In the world beyond my little town of Brookfield there is a dreadful war raging that is setting brother against brother and bringing sorrow and grief upon the entire nation. I would see all men and women free from social and political bondage, but what will be the cost...and who will ultimately pay the price? One thing I do know and that is, I can no longer remain silent. More and more women are raising their voices and demanding to be heard. The time has come for me to join their ranks.

More anon, LFW

A reader's guide to
British words and colloquialisms
for American readers

Aga .... a popular, very high-end brand of kitchen stove
Bacon and chip butty ......bacon and chip (French fry) sandwich
Bangers and mash ... sausages & mashed potatoes fried together
Besom .... a kind of broom, but often refers to a witchy
        personality, usually female.
Biro .... ball point pen
Biscuits .... cookies
Brolly .... umbrella
Cardi .... Cardigan or other sweater with buttons up the front
Chivvy .... encourage
Cooker .... stove
Crisps .... potato chips
Dickey .... not right
Elevenes ...... mid-morning break, often coffee rather than tea
Faffin' about .... wasting time
Gets out of her/his pram .... bent out of shape, really bothered
           about something
Get wrong .... be in trouble
Give it a bit of welly .... put some muscle into it or
         when driving, to "step on it"
In good nick .... feeling well
Knickers .... .ladies underpants
Loo .... toilet
Not half ...."You've got that right."
Poorly .... not feeling well
Paracetemol .... pain killer like Tylenol
Peckish .... hungry
Peelie-wally .... looking ill
Pissed as a newt .... very, very drunk
Plaster .... Band-Aid or other adhesive bandage
Prezzie .... gift or present

Pudding ....dessert, a sweet after a meal
Sponge .... light airy cake like you might use for
a jelly roll, think sponge-cake
Summat .... something
Tablets .... pills
Taking the mickey.................. pulling my leg, making a joke
Tenner ....ten pound note, (ten dollar bill)
Torch .... flashlight
Wellies .... see below!
Wellingtons .... tall rubber boots
Wooly Jumper .... pullover sweater
Y'daft brush .... term of affection, rather like silly fool

Sticky Toffee Pudding
--the easy American version that tastes (almost) as good as the original

When you try this, you'll see why Olympia flipped over it. My husband and I were married in England, and we served it at our wedding reception.

The Sponge (the thing that soaks up that fantastic sauce!)

Prepare a **spice cake** or basic **yellow cake** mix according to directions, but use strong coffee instead of milk or water. Add 1 cup of finely chopped dates which have been blended into a puree using some of the coffee. Bake in a well-greased 9 x 13 baking pan. When done remove from oven and let sit 5 minutes. While still hot, cut into serving size pieces (usually 12-16) and leave in the pan. Pour warm toffee sauce over the hot cake in the pan, making sure to drizzle it into the cuts you've just made and along the sides.

Toffee Sauce

2-1/2 cups heavy cream
1 cup light brown sugar
1 stick sweet unsalted butter
Sprinkle of salt
½ to 1 cup chopped pecans (optional but fantastic!)

Mix everything except the pecans in a saucepan, stirring constantly until everything is melted and gorgeous. Add the pecans and pour the hot sauce over the cake/sponge. Serve warm to hot or reheat just before serving. Usually served with unwhipped heavy cream called pouring cream or whipped cream or vanilla ice cream, or sometimes with Bird's Custard, an English instant custard mix available in many American grocery stores.

Meet Author Judith Campbell

Rev. Dr. Judith Campbell is an ordained Unitarian Universalist minister and the author of many books and articles. She has published children's stories and poetry, as well as numerous essays on the arts, religion and spirituality. Her "Mission Mysteries" series is her latest endeavor.

She holds a PhD in The Arts and Religious Studies and a Master of Arts in Fine Arts, and she offers writing workshops and religious retreats nationally and internationally.

When she isn't traveling and teaching, she spends her time in Plymouth, Massachusetts, and on the island of Martha's Vineyard with her husband and best friend, Chris Stokes, a "Professional Englishman," together with their annoyingly intelligent cats, Katie and Simon.

To learn more about The Sinister Minister or to invite her to lead a writing workshop, preach at your church or speak at your library or book group, please visit her website at www.judithcampbell-holymysteries.com. "Rev Judy" loves to talk to her readers, and book club guides, as well as the answers to frequently asked questions, can also be found here.

~

Also in the Olympia Brown Mystery Series

A Deadly Mission
An Unspeakable Mission
A Despicable Mission
An Unholy Mission
A Predatory Mission

*Preview of the seventh Olympia Brown Mystery
coming from Mainly Murder Press in 2014*

A Singular Mission
by Judith Campbell

Prologue

Rev. Olympia Brown was sitting at her desk in the office of the Salt Rock Village Fellowship of Cape Cod. Hanging on the doorknob was a gift bag with her name on it. Seeing it there, she recalled a warning from her days in seminary. The professor had looked over his glasses at the ministers in training and said, "Watch out for the note takers and the gift givers. They can spell trouble. You need to handle them with kid-gloves, and you need to watch your back."

Pink and red tissue paper was spilling out of the top of the latest "little something," and the attached card was signed with a heart and a smiley face. She knew it would likely be some sort of little trinket or useless knick-knack, the kind she particularly loathed, such as a statue of a sad-eyed kid in a nightgown or one more goddamn angel with a sappy message about how God is watching over you etched into the bottom. Only God wasn't the only one watching over her. A lonely, unhappy woman named Amelia Goodale had attached herself to Olympia like a homeless kitten.

Chapter 1

Olympia Brown remembered when she had accepted the position of supply minister in the picturebook white steepled church on upper Cape Cod. It was inconveniently located between the two major roads, Routes 6 and 6A, and because of that was conveniently ignored by most of the summer visitors.

The regular minister was on sabbatical, and they needed someone to preach on Sundays and be available for pastoral care. The appointment started on the fifteenth of January and was scheduled to continue through the ides of April, just three months. There was little to do other than preach on Sundays, visit the sick and the elderly, and hold things together until the settled minister returned. "It will be a piece of cake," said the District Supervisor. She could do it with her eyes shut.

She'd been told that once before by the same man, and that time she'd landed on the island of Martha's Vineyard with the bad end of a gun pointed in her direction.

"Why don't you tell me the whole story?"

"There isn't one that I know of." He smiled. "Look at it this way; it's a great opportunity to enjoy a short ministry in a healthy, family-sized church in a charming location. You'll make a little money, and they'll have a minister they can count on."

"In the dead of winter," she added.

"But the Cape never gets as much snow as the other side of the bridge," he wheedled.

"Except when it does, Zak, and I know, it always melts faster. Tell me more. You need to convince me."

In the end he accomplished his mission. Olympia signed the contract, agreeing to begin work two weeks after Christmas, and within days the phone calls started.

"Hi, Reverend Brown? My name is Amelia Goodale. I'm a member of Salt Rock, and I just wanted to say welcome to the Fellowship on behalf of all of us and tell you how happy we all are to have a woman in the pulpit for a change."

"Why, thank you, Amelia. It's very kind of you, and it makes me feel very welcome. Was there anything else you wanted to talk about?"

Olympia was absent-mindedly stroking her cat Cadeau, who had stretched himself out in a patch of winter sunlight on her desk next to the computer.

"Oh, no, not right now anyway, Reverend, but it's sweet of you to ask. They said you were friendly and easy to talk to, and I guess you really are. I volunteered to be one of the ushers on the day you start, so I'll there to welcome and introduce you."

"That will be lovely. I'll be looking forward to meeting you in person, Amelia. Thank you for calling."

"Goodbye, Reverend."

Olympia should have paid more attention to what it was about the conversation that had made her feel uncomfortable. She really should have, because if she had, things might have gone very differently.

Within a week of Olympia starting the job, Amelia began bringing little gifts. At first it was just a cup of coffee.

"I was on my way over here, and I stopped for coffee, and I remembered you drink coffee, so I got two. You don't mind, do you?"

There was no possible answer to that other than, "Of course not, it was very thoughtful. Thank you." Olympia really did like coffee, and this was fresh and hot. She pushed away the twice-warmed-over stuff she'd brought from home and reached for the paper cup.

"Um, Reverend?"

"Yes, Amelia?"

"Could I make an appointment to talk with you sometime? There are some things I probably should talk about with someone, but I never felt comfortable with Rev. Sommers. Maybe it's because he's a man, and I prefer women ministers, but he never acted as though he really cared about what I had to say. You're different. I can see that already."

Red flags started flapping all over the office, but fortunately only Olympia could see them.

"When were you thinking?"

"Well, I'm here right now, and I've got a few minutes, so I thought maybe…."

Olympia pulled a datebook out of her handbag and set it on her desk. "I have some time on Thursday at eleven. Could you come back then?"

Amelia looked crestfallen. "I hoped … I mean, it won't take very long, but I suppose if you're busy…"

She waited for Olympia to relent and invite her to sit down, but it didn't happen.

"I've left this morning open for drop-ins, Amelia. I'm sensing you might want a more private conversation. I'm afraid we'd be interrupted, and that wouldn't be fair to you, and I wouldn't like that. I want to be able to give you my full attention."

"You do?" The wary and petulant frown vanished, and suddenly she was all smiles once again.

"So can you make it on Thursday?"

"Gee, I don't have my calendar with me. Can I call in and let you know?"

"You can leave a message on the church phone. I'll be sure to check it."

"I could call you at home." A hopeful smile.

"I'd rather you called here. That way I'll be sure to get it. My husband isn't the best of message takers."

"I'll try, Reverend. It depends on when I get home. So you're married?"

Olympia smiled and nodded. "That's fine, just let me know, okay?"

"Sure, Reverend, and if there's anything you need help with, just give me a call. I think it's important to support the minister." She lowered her voice. "Not everyone here does, so be careful— and you didn't hear me say that."

"Thank you, Amelia."

When she left, Olympia sat staring at the door and shaking her head. Poor thing, she thought. She'd encountered her kind before, pathetically in need of attention and approval from the person in charge—the teacher, the parent, the coach, or in this case the minister. The trick was finding the right balance, enough attention and affirmation to let her know she was a valued member of the community but not so much that she formed an unhealthy attachment. Balance and boundaries were the key words here, and she was very familiar with them. Easy to say, not so easy to maintain. She knew that, too.

"Reverend?"

Olympia looked up. Amelia Goodale was back.

"There's something else I meant to tell you."

Coming in 2014 from Mainly Murder Press
www.MainlyMurderPress.com

CPSIA information can be obtained at www.ICGtesting.com
Printed in the USA
BVOW01s1230040614

354973BV00001BD/1/P